I Never Came

to You in White

I Never Came to You in White

to You in White

A NOVEL

JUDITH FARR

A Peter Davison Book

HOUGHTON MIFFLIN COMPANY

BOSTON   NEW YORK

1996

1 — 3 8 8 4

For information about permission to reproduce selections from
this book, write to Permissions, Houghton Mifflin Company,
215 Park Avenue South, New York, New York 10003.

For information about this and other Houghton Mifflin
trade and reference books and multimedia products, visit
The Bookstore at Houghton Mifflin on the World Wide Web
at http://www.hmco.com/trade/.

Library of Congress Cataloging-in-Publication Data
Farr, Judith.
I never came to you in white : a novel / Judith Farr
p.   cm.
"A Peter Davison book."
ISBN 0-395-78840-4
1. Dickinson, Emily, 1830–1886 — Correspondence — Fiction.
2. Women poets, American — 19th century — Fiction.   I. Title.
PS3556.A73312   1996
813'.54 — dc20   96-11654   CIP

Printed in the United States of America

QUM 10 9 8 7 6 5 4 3 2 1

Book design by Melodie Wertelet

Selections from *The Poems of Emily Dickinson:* Reprinted by
permission of the publishers and the Trustees of Amherst College
from *The Poems of Emily Dickinson,* Thomas H. Johnson, ed.,
Cambridge, Mass.: The Belknap Press of Harvard University Press,
Copyright © 1951, 1955, 1979, 1983 by the President and Fellows
of Harvard College.

For George, with love

"What would you do with me
if I came 'in white'?"

·

— Emily Dickinson,
Letter to "Master," about 1861

I Never Came

to You in White

I do not, cannot, call you anything yet; I am not sure yet what you are to me. But you are rooted in my deepest heart. You have been for a year.

I must go to Miss Lyon's tomorrow. Father insists. But I know that I do not leave you in this room when I go. I know that you will follow me.

I will speak to you always in my *real* voice: not in the polished syllables I must use for others — the bright thin talk of the tea table, the sewing circle and the classroom. Nor will I speak to you in that rhetorical voice I use to keep strangers away. To you, I will speak in the hard plain tongue of my Soul.

You will not mind if I am passionate!

Do not fail to enter the buggy with me tomorrow. Do not fail!

*M*y dear Mr. Higginson:

Are you too occupied to hear my voice?

I am a stranger to you and so you may not understand why I take the liberty of addressing you. But an old woman like myself, sixty-seven momentarily, cannot linger too much longer in this world, and I *must* ease my conscience with respect to someone who concerns you. Someone who has *deeply* concerned you, judging by the Preface you have written to her poems.

I speak of Emily Dickinson.

I was her teacher almost fifty years ago. Things happened between us, and I did things — things I cannot forget.

I am told that you are not only a journalist, but an ordained minister. (By the way, I have long admired your pieces in the *Atlantic Monthly*. Very affecting, I always find them, especially that essay called "The Procession of the Flowers." It's the rare man who appreciates flowers!) My problem is of a spiritual nature. I know that you are a good person, I can tell that from your writing style — so self-effacing and wholesome. I feel that you will want to help me.

But if you are to help me, I must tell you a long story. I entreat you, will you hear it? If so, will you write me to that effect?

Yours sincerely,
Margaret Mann

*D*ear Mamma,

You will be pleased no doubt to learn that I had an uneventful journey from our own blessed home to the sacred portals of Miss Lyon's, where Religion still flourishes and Learning follows suit. On my arrival, several of the young ladies I took classes with last year were awaiting me in the Recreation Parlors, and, Mamma, we had many high jinks in the very first golden moments alone! Sarah Albright has put up her hair, although she is only sixteen! Now, Mamma, you would never have let me do so. You recall how you did forbid it, saying it was never right to "hasten Nature" and seem more grown-up than your years. But *her* Mamma obviously disagrees with you! Miss Jenny Ridley from Charleston, S.C., says she was the "reigning belle" of that city all summer long, but, as Livia Coleman whispered to me under her breath while Miss Jenny boasted, "Charleston is a no-account village full of puffed-up simpletons." If one were voted the Belle of a serious city like Boston or even a sober town like Amherst, now *that* would be a compliment! New Englanders don't tell lies!

Speaking of Amherst, Cousin Emily Dickinson has arrived with many boxes and books. She is the only girl on our corridor who has come away to school with her own books. (Isn't it enough that we are burdened with Miss Lyon's choices?) Some of the other young ladies watched her in dumb amazement as she un-wrapped her Testament, a lexicon, an atlas, and several parcels that were full of what I am afraid to report are "novels" — she confessed it — written by foreigners. One is called *The Old Curiosity Shop* by that Englishman named "Dickins"; she has been reading it every chance she gets. Maybe she likes it because the Englishman's name sounds like hers.

You asked me to say right away if I like Emily, Mamma. Of course I *want* very much to like her and maybe I shall. It has been so many years since we met. I wish it had not been so many or that you had invited her to visit us before deciding that I must be her sponsor here and share her room. I know I should not complain, Mamma, but I would have preferred a girl my own age for a companion, not a younger one like Emily — a girl who is new to the Seminary besides! I do recall what a dear lonely little thing Emily seemed when we were small and she came to Monson to stay while my Aunt Emily was sick. I can still picture her sitting sorrowfully on the stairs outside the kitchen, all alone and staring at her little boots until Papa went out to her and picked her up and hugged her hard. She was worried that Aunt Emily was going to die, remember? But after we cheered her up, she turned merry and liked to laugh and tell stories. That was the year she and I made a lovely tree house for our dollies.

But Emily seems different now. She's very courteous, Mamma, and she receives my advice respectfully as befits a girl who is a whole year younger than myself. Yet somehow I fear she won't settle down and be happy and normal like the rest of us. There's something *strange* about her.

Do you know what she told me this morning? She said she hasn't joined the church yet, despite all the eloquence of the Revival, because she "can't give up the world"! Now, Mamma, don't that beat all? What "world" would that girl know about?

Your loving grand-daughter,
Emily Norcross

*M*y dear Miss Margaret Mann,

It was with great joy that I read the name "Emily Dickinson" in your letter of some weeks ago. I beg your forgiveness for not having replied to it sooner. My beloved wife has been ill and when at first her ailment seemed serious, anxiety so overwhelmed me that I was quite unable to write so much as my signature. Mercifully, she is now recovered. But then the book I had set aside (its title may amuse you: *Common Sense About Women*) claimed my attention. It is to be published in a few weeks and I had been given proofs to read. My silence, however, is no measure of my interest in you or, more precisely, in the contents of your letter!

You cannot know this, dear Miss Mann, but your letter contained a phrase, "Are you too occupied," that nearly stopped my heart. When I read it, thirty years fell away and I was returned to that morning of April sixteenth, 1862, when I stood in the post office in Worcester, Massachusetts, and took delivery of a most remarkable letter. The letter contained — how well I remember! I have it still, still re-read it, and am struck by it again — the most abrupt of salutations. No "Dear ———," no "My dear ———." Just "Mr. Higginson," like a thunder-clap. And then this arresting sentence: "Are you too deeply occupied to say if my Verse is alive?"

In those days, I had just begun to write my essays for the *Atlantic*, one of which you kindly commended. Because so many would-be poets wrote to me asking for advice, and because the *Atlantic* was tired of receiving manuscripts from tyros, the editors had urged me to offer the public some counsel about writing. That April I published my "Letter to a Young Contributor." After Miss Emily Dickinson — once, oh marvelous even to contemplate, your pupil! — read it, she sent me that first of many treasured letters. She also enclosed four poems, so I could judge whether her poetry "breathed." I see myself still, a busy, lively, well-meaning youth with three newspapers under his arm, standing stock-still in the post office amid a throng of people mailing packages to the soldiers, trying to read one of those poems. The poem was hard for me to read. All her poems were — stunning, elusive, brilliant. But unorthodox!

The poem began "We play at paste." Yet I knew it was not about its apparent subject, how pearls are made. I recognized that the writer was telling me that *she* knew how to make pearls, that her poem was a pearl. What the Bible calls "a pearl of great price," perhaps. I can only imagine what she may have been like as a student, but I can report that as a poet Miss Dickinson was very daring.

Oh yes, my dear Miss Mann, I should be most happy to hear anything you may say about Emily Dickinson. Nothing you could write would be too long. No one could possibly imagine how much I miss my dear friend, now that she has — in the words of her favorite

Emily Brontë — "put on Immortality." That is, if she could ever be said to have put it off! I always thought Miss Dickinson came so clearly from Heaven that some of its light shone forth from her eyes.

Very cordially yours,
T. W. Higginson

*D*ear Mr. Higginson,

I thank you heartily for replying to my letter. I have stifled myself a long while because it *hurts* me to remember what I must tell you. I need help, I need grace, I need light! When a Quaker woman like me knows she has lost her inner light, it is impossible for her not to seek guidance, even from a Unitarian like yourself.

I think I should commence by giving you my very first impression of Emily Dickinson. If you think *your* first encounter with her poetry was challenging, you will be amazed to hear of my initial contact with her! I met her on the morning I began my life as a teacher of rhetoric. My first task was to read the roll, and there were so many names to call out that they were all a blur to me. I remembered Emily's later, only because of her startling behavior. Miss Lyon was very strict about form. And so every day we teachers had to get up on a small dais in Seminary Hall and first see to it that the young ladies were well combed and well washed, standing in perfect rows, and then call out their names. It seemed easy, but, like everything else in life, it wasn't.

I prayed that morning because I was so anxious. I prayed, "O God of Our Fathers, enable your humble servant Margaret Mann to rise above her pettiness and frailty to serve you in the capacity of writing mistress. Help me to draw the hearts in my care to your mercy and love." This was the prayer that my father, a Quaker minister, had written out for me before I left Springfield to serve under Miss Lyon. And I know he meant it to calm and steady me, but it did not.

I entered the Hall shivering, not just from the September chill. I seemed to myself too young for schoolmistressing and, as the sun streamed through the tall windows so radiantly, I wished I were far away and alone by myself in my mother's orchard. There were, I thought, too many names, and the rows of girls in their brown or blue or claret merino gowns and their white or yellow pinafores, their braids, their cameos at the throat, bored me already. As I knew very well, it is a great sin to be bored. But I plucked up my courage, looked at my list, and spoke the names distinctly with what Father would have called "spirit."

The names were as old-fashioned as stir-about pudding — not like the smart Frenchified ones of today. I can still see the list:

> Laetitia Partington Snowe
> Frances Maria Upson
> Anna Robinson
> Fanny Arms
> Georgiana McElwain
> Sarah Cairns
> Julia Dame Bodfish
> Katharina Cobleigh
> Nettie Coolidge
> Ella Swenarton
> Lena Aldritch
> Emily Norcross

Malvina Stanton
Sarah Wright
and Emily Dickinson.

I do not think, even now, that I should be blamed for not recognizing, on that first day of school, whom and what I had before me. "Emily Dickinson" is a commonplace name in western Massachusetts. There are hundreds of Dickinsons. Father claims they think of themselves as a distinguished group, descended from some medieval French knight called De Kenson. But the Dickinson we knew in Springfield was only a black-smith. "Emily" is the most ordinary of names besides. I don't know how many Emilys I myself went to school with. And this Emily was thin and plain with not a single pretty feature or grace. (Well, she had almost translucently fair skin, it's true, and when she smiled, her lip curled in a merry fashion.) The first time I set eyes on her, she looked like the ghost of a ghost in her gray dress. I found myself wondering how a ghost would reply as I went down the call-out list, but the ghost never answered me. When I said her name, she just kept staring off into the distance with that peculiar thinking look on her face. I was irritated. It was the first of many times she made me irritated. So I sputtered, "Miss, do you have another name in mind, or are you going to learn to answer to your own?" And the bag-gage looked straight at me then, bright as a sixpence, and said, right out in front of all the others, "I do have a private name for myself, Ma'am, though I am sorry to have missed your saying mine. I was daydreaming. You see, I always think of myself as Eve."

Eve! Not a girl in a million would come up with such a name. Here in our school dedicated to preparing the soul for Eternity; a school that sends out more women to the missions than any other institution in New England! Eve: the name of the original sinner, a name to be forgotten! I should have guessed right then that she would cleverly defy us all. And yet, how could I guess? I could not have supposed that that pale slight minx would, in fifty years time, become the celebrated personage whose name I read with embarrassment yesterday on that book of poems you brought out and wrote your Preface to: *"Emily Dickinson."*

I think, perhaps, re-reading your letter, Mr. Higginson, that you and I knew two different people. Your letter, expressing such admiration for Emily, depressed me. And although this letter starts bravely enough, I find myself too weary to continue it. After all, you have come out publicly as Emily Dickinson's friend and mentor. I was in a way her enemy and adversary. If you really knew all that took place, you would not *want* me to correspond with you, I think!

Yrs,
Margaret Mann

I opened the window after Cousin Emily was asleep, but you did not come to me. I left it open long enough to smell the fields at home and see the light curve down from the stars. Still you did not come! I called to you. And still —

It is colder here than I could ever have supposed. The cold has hands. Summer has truly folded her miracle and we are knifed about by bitter winds. I will have to go on here. Unless I can fall very ill, Father will not let me go home. It would not be for Father's sake I would wish to go home. It is Austin *he* loves. It's not even for Vinnie, my sister. She is sweet, you may know, but we speak a different language. It is for You: your shining eyes, your paradisal Face — glowing at me!

I thought I heard you say you would follow. We are not allowed to lock our doors here so you may come at any time.

Do not desert me in this Wilderness!

*M*y very dear Abiah,

Why have you not sent me an affectionate epistle?

In my last, I wrote to you that I was leaving for South Hadley Seminary and told you all my airy schemes for success here. When Sabra Johnson visited you at Feeding Hills, she said you admitted to having received many letters from me and answering not one of them! Yet I recall, Abiah, when you were so eager for the slightest one of my notes that you would send me an answer, quick as the bounding (and boundless) birds.

Do write to me. For although there is always something interesting to me in Self-Denial — sometimes I imagine it is more rewarding than Pleasure; it makes the mind work! — I cannot always do without. Love, I can *never* do without.

The ceaseless flight of the seasons is such a solemn thought. When I last saw you, it was the first of April and we kissed farewell in a shower of lilac bloom as you entered your carriage in my Father's drive. Now it is October, the dying of the Year. And soon again, it will be spring. Perhaps you will visit me then!

Write and tell me all your news.

Your affectionate
Emily Elizabeth Dickinson

$\mathcal{M}$y dear Miss Mann,

I am sure that in Emily Dickinson, you and I knew the *same* person. For (to venture upon the kind of pun she often enjoyed) Miss Dickinson was *unique!*

But I am both distressed and puzzled by some of your observations about Miss Emily. I can only suppose that, as a very young person yourself, you may have exaggerated the degree of her gentle mischievousness. For that is what I take her association of herself with Eve to be, a kind of mischief!

It did have its origin in her beliefs, of course. She always judged that the chief characteristic of our First Female Parent was her desire for knowledge. We once discussed it. According to Genesis and according to Milton, it was Eve's hunger to *know* that made her disobedient. During her life, Miss Emily was often censured on account of her own passion for knowledge, so she felt rather sympathetic, you see, to Eve. She had many such ideas, rather iconoclastic, perhaps, for a mid-Victorian gentlewoman, but charming.

One reason for my compliance with Mrs. Todd's request that I assist her in editing the *Poems* is that I believe, as Emily Dickinson did, that women should be allowed more freedom of expression. Though Miss Emily never seized her audience in her lifetime, being unwilling, finally, to print her rare words, she did believe in women thinking as freely as men. There, too, she was like Eve. Do not be hard on yourself, my dear lady. I am eager to hear more and ready to be of any assistance.

Yrs, *T. W. Higginson*

$\mathcal{D}$ear Mr. Higginson,

I thank you for answering me so promptly. You are a famous man, I know, with many obligations. I am a "Nobody," as your friend's poem so jauntily puts it — "I'm Nobody, who are you, are you Nobody too?" Very clever and disarming. And, of course, completely false. Miss Dickinson thought a great deal of herself. Even as a child, she was an egotist.

If I am to explain it all, Mr. Higginson, I must tell you about my life, too, in those days and about the common life of the school, which was not untroubled.

Miss Lyon had set her Seminary amid lovely environs. I would look out my window in the morning before any of the students were up and stare out at the sky, shadowy and mysterious, as if it had a secret to tell. I would lean upon the windowsill in my wrapper and watch while the darkness gave way, like a person holding something to his chest who was having it taken from him slowly. The quiet before the rising bell was precious to me. In all the twenty years I was at Miss Lyon's — she died, actually, not long after I came and then the seminary was called, simply, "Mount Holyoke" — I never learned to put up with the pupils' noise. It was not that they were disorderly, bad-natured, or ill-mannered on the whole; but girls *will* chatter and giggle! Miss Lyon tried to discourage them by imposing Silent Rule in the corridors and everywhere but in a pupil's room or during recreation, dining hall, and Botany Walk.

But the little devils (some of them really *were*, I could smell the fuming pitch) whispered behind their hands or under their desks. And some — even Emily Dickinson on occasion! — passed notes and letters to each other. I would hear the rustle of the paper in the recipients' hands while I was at the blackboard with my back to them. So I loved the early morning peace at Mount Holyoke, before the tumult inevitably commenced and the bell rang and I had to lose myself as a person and lapse into being a disciplinarian: The Writing Mistress.

I remember very well that first term when Emily Dickinson came to us. We were both new, she and I, and it was the Fall of 1847. That was the year the Revival came to Holyoke, and no matter how strong in the Lord a girl or woman might be she could feel herself just a leaf going down the wind when preachers like Mr. Edwards Amasa Park or President Hitchcock from Amherst spoke out on Human Depravity or Entering by the Strait Gate. Miss Lyon invited a local minister or an "educator-notable" to come on Sundays for the two-hour service in the morning and the two-hour evening one. When they couldn't come, she spoke herself, on "Self-Denial," it might be, or "Hope" or "Faith" or "The World Well-Lost for Christ." I see her still, with her mild, broad face, bad skin, and white turban in the style of the former age, mounting to a pulpit in the chapel, smoothing her bodice, looking round benignly and then launching into words of fire and brimstone. Although we were a school, and Miss Lyon referred to us as "One Family," her real purpose was to convert, to make the girls "declare for Christ," if they had not already done so in their local churches. She went about it with noble fury. She used to say "I teach chemistry and Christ." And although she was kind enough, she was so afraid her lambs would not be saved that she gave them little peace till they acknowledged the Good Shepherd. In the Fall of 1847, there were revivals all over New England. But the one we had at the Seminary was as thorough-going and scarifying as any I've ever known. Squire Dickinson and that silly plaintive wife of his — not much of a model for a bright girl like Emily — sent their little "Eve" right into it.

Emily Dickinson had come from Amherst to South Hadley in an open buggy, and passing over the windy landscape must have given her a cold. She had a racking cough that first day she entered my classroom, which was on the north side of the building and heated only by a small stove. (Since Miss Lyon sent missionary wives to wildest China, she wanted them accustomed to discomfort). Somehow — and this is the *strangest* thing — I found myself, after that first annoyance at roll call, *drawn* to her, as if we two shared an understanding or were related in some way. (This feeling did not last!) I watched her slight form as she shrank from the chilly windows and I placed her as close to the fire as I could. Doing so, I discovered, was not wise because fires delighted Emily — she found drama in the blaze and pathos in the embers, and would be henceforth heedless of any of my observations on the correct use of the participle or on punctuation. She was lost in reverie.

To tell the truth, I was somewhat like her. I had

no idea that even as a sixteen-year-old child she was in the habit of writing verse. But I myself wanted — no, *yearned* — to be a poetess. Of course such an idea among Quakers is regarded as next door to sinful. With us, there can be no music, no dancing, no false stories that the world calls "novels," and no poetry, except for John Milton's. It's strange, I suppose, because we do believe in what our founder Mr. Fox called the "voice within." But that voice can be lifted only in prayer. Father would have forbidden me to write poetry. He was not happy when I became a rhetoric teacher, so great was his distrust of words! I had to keep myself, though, for we were not well-off at home. Well, Mr. Higginson, sometimes — as I was talking to some dolt-ish girl about rhetoric — I might glance at the fire my-self and build palaces of art therein.

Emily Dickinson was at first assigned to the Junior Class or "form." At Miss Lyon's there were two forms after that: the Middle Class, to which she aspired, and the Senior, which she never reached. Her parents took her home after two semesters — very peculiar, we all thought it. The fact that she was entering my classroom meant that she had passed her examinations to enter the Middle Class. They took three days in her case. I heard from Miss Chapin, Miss Lyon's assistant, that she had done wonderfully in the literary exercise and even in science and history. But it was all, Miss Chapin said, quite a drain on Emily Dickinson, and not because of her cold but because she was so obviously alarmed at being watched. (Final examinations are open to the public and a great many in South and East Hadley attend, sitting in rows before the pupils, who stand on the dais in Seminary Hall and answer to spoken questions.) Apparently, her voice hardly rose above a whisper and that so irritated the postmaster, Mr. Cobleigh, Katharina's father, that he barked, "Speak up, young woman! If your father's paying to educate you as if you were good as a boy, give him his money's worth." And after that, Emily got a little fiery and declaimed her exercise on Ecclesiastical History like a regular Jonathan Edwards, with a gimlet eye for old Mr. Cobleigh. I could tell you many stories like that one about Emily Dickinson, stories that the braver girls in the school feasted on for years after she left us. But I must return to her first day with me.

The Writing Mistress for the Middle Class does two things: she teaches Milton's *Paradise Lost,* which Miss Lyon found spiritually as well as mentally uplifting, and she instructs the class in the elements of composition. Emily Dickinson had prepared at Amherst Academy, on whose plan Miss Lyon founded her own school. Thus, even had she not been precocious — exceptional, really — she might have excelled above the other pupils. But the degree to which she would excel and the manner of her excellence: ah, we never could have predicted that! To say that her brilliance created envy, rancorous and deep, among some of the girls is not even to approach describing it. To my everlasting shame, it made *me* envious as well. For how do you teach someone who sees where you are blind; who, like a tiny ferret or slim whippet or beautiful leaping fawn, flashes into a light you never supposed was there, while you yourself are trudging along in mud, in darkness? It takes a saint to put up with genius. Of course, I was and am no saint.

Furthermore, it was not at first clear to me that Emily Dickinson was really capable of the imaginative work she very quickly began to turn in to me. I am not naturally suspicious. But when I read her first composition I thought she had copied it, gone to the school library and helped herself to a few phrases written by someone else. After all, she was just a girl from Amherst! The essay she wrote was incredibly sophisticated. But had I paid more attention that very first day, even to the independent way she sat and gazed — out the window or at her oddly plump little hands or at the tiny print of a little book she surreptitiously inserted within the covers of Phelps's *Rhetoric* — I would never have been so foolish as to doubt she wrote that essay or, later, all those irreverent, scandalous poems. One thing is certain: in Emily Dickinson, Miss Lyon's belief that the imagination led one astray was perfectly illustrated.

On that first day the teachers were expected to prepare the girls for their parts in the Revival. Miss Lyon told us in the teachers' room that morning that she knew not everyone in the Seminary would immediately come forward and make Christ their portion. She said it sorrowfully but firmly, clutching her immaculate white dress by the folds at the sides, as she always did when thoughtful. Miss Lyon knew as well as any of us that the flesh is weak. Indeed, I will never forget her telling me, when she took me on, that she thought herself forever in danger of being "an enemy to God and His cause." Why? Because she so loved reading! Reading was encouraged, you see, but never in the place of prayer, and Miss Lyon confided in me that she had once actually preferred Shakespeare to the Scriptures and had to "overcome" it! Well, it is true that, as my father has said, Shakespeare's vocabulary is often wicked and his morals were certainly corrupt. When I think of that "Dark Lady" of the sonnets, I realize that he was well acquainted with the Devil. Nevertheless, if you like poetry, Shakespeare can be thrilling despite his wickedness. I confess that the balcony scene in *Romeo and Juliet* made me wish, once, for a man. I don't mean a husband; I mean a *man*. (Pray do not despise me for my candor!)

After the girls seated themselves in our classrooms, Miss Lyon explained, we were to sing a hymn with them and next we were to demand that "those without hope" of eternal salvation would immediately declare themselves. The names of girls without hope would then be inscribed on a list nailed to the side door of the chapel. They would be ordered to go regularly to private prayer meetings in Miss Lyon's own rooms. Everything would be done, including special sessions with the Revival preachers, to force such hard-hearted girls to see the error of their ways and to love the good Christ who died for them! As a Quaker, I am not accustomed to so much discipline from without. I prefer the "inner light" and no intrusions on the work of conscience. But in 1847, I knew it was safer to bow before the Revival frenzy. I did not want to lose my employment. I could not go home to be a drain on Father. I knew I was being watched. We all were.

The hymn I chose to lead my pupils in singing was

Martin Luther's "Eine feste Burg." As it turned out, Emily Dickinson knew that hymn in the original German, which she had studied at Amherst Academy. But certainly she displayed no fondness for it. I can still picture the room where we gathered that day: a nice whitewashed room (everything was always plain at Holyoke) with only the wood-burning stove, my teacher's desk, and the pupils' smaller desks and tall hard-back chairs, and one steel engraving of George Washington. I spoke some words about Satan and his lewd efforts to seduce Christian souls. And I started up the hymn as loudly as I could.

Emily Dickinson began her career as a brilliant oddity among us almost at once, just after we had sung the last verse. It was a verse Miss Lyon especially preferred, because Reverend Luther is very specific in it about the Devil's powers. I can still hear the girls singing in their wavering sopranos:

> And though this world, with devils filled,
> Should threaten to undo us,
> We will not fear, for God hath willed
> His truth to triumph through us;
> The prince of darkness grim —
> We tremble not for him;
> His rage we can endure;
> For O, his doom is sure;
> One little word shall fell him.

Emily's cold, I thought, was what was making her so pale as we sang. But by the time we reached the "world, with devils filled," she was white as a corpse and had to lean against her chair, unable to stand upright.

"Miss Dickinson," I said as soon as we stopped, "what is the matter?"

Now, the interesting thing is that Emily was truly shy, that was no pretense. But if you asked her a direct question — about an idea or a feeling, say — she gave you an answer quick as a blaze striking up from dry wood.

"Oh, ma'am," she choked, as if she were desperate, "that hymn makes me feel wild, as if I had seen a spirit. I tremble when I think that my fate is sealed. I feel that I am sailing upon the brink of an awful precipice, from which I cannot escape and over which I fear my tiny boat will soon glide if I do not receive help from above. You mean to try and persuade us to be Christians. Well, I was once about to declare for Christ and I never enjoyed such perfect peace and happiness as in that short time in which I felt I found my Savior. But one by one my old habits returned. The world allured me and I listened to her siren voice. Oh, I cannot give up the world! I *cannot* give up Shakespeare and Byron and my flowers! The devil must claim his dark child, for I am not able to care for anybody or anything but what I love! And I cannot say truly that right now I love God. I do not feel that I know Him well enough for love. I am so ashamed!"

Well, I couldn't tell if she was speaking the truth or not, her language was so . . . *extreme!* Boats and precipices, sirens! *Shakespeare!* (The last was so dangerous for her — as a student, as a *soul* — I winced to think of it!) And I cannot describe how annoying and disconcerting it was to have to put up with such rubbishy sentimentality on my first day in a classroom.

"Miss Dickinson," I snapped, "this is not a theatrical show. All that is required here is the simple acknowledgment that you are a fallen being like the rest of us and in need of God's mercy; that naught but God matters to you and that you will love Him above all folk, do His will and walk in His ways all the days of your life. That said and done, you can resume your studies like everyone else."

"Oh, but it is not simple, Miss Mann, to promise to walk always in God's ways. Is anyone sure what they are? Do you think the God who ordered Abraham to kill Isaac is the same God as the one who claimed to love all men? Dr. Hitchcock tells me I am a worm. But I cannot feel . . . wormlike. And I am so easily excited. I experience transport when ministers preach on sublime subjects like the Resurrection. And then I fancy I believe. Indeed, I am in a positive fever, ma'am, to believe! But when I am honest, I know that it is only their *words* that have moved me. 'One little word,' Luther says, 'shall fell him.' That is myself, ma'am, I am one who is felled by words."

And then she smiled, that strange elusive Emily Dickinson smile, as I got to calling it, where her long upper lip seemed to disappear into her cheeks but her teeth never showed. It was as if she were revealing and yet hiding herself all at once.

And then she began to cough, that thin little bosomless chest heaving up and down under her gray gown. Except for her strong, well-developed hands, she was very thin. But she had red hair and all the life of her being seemed to lie in that flaming hair, in her high quizzical voice, and of course on her lips, when she spoke. Otherwise, she looked physically wraithlike, at least to me, for I have always been a big buxom woman and glad to be. I am a no-nonsense person for all my desire to write verse. My model for a poet is a plain commonsensical body like Helen Hunt Jackson. She knew Emily Dickinson, isn't that so? But I hear she never had much influence over her. Mrs. Jackson was a very successful writer, was she not? And you know better than I, Mr. Higginson, that Emily was so eccentric, her neighbors called her "The Myth." Mrs. Jackson had her feet on the ground. And she had a sound plump figure that showed she had.

"'Felled by words,' are you?" I said then, as kindly as I could — for after all I meant to be kind. "Good! Perhaps, Emily, you would pen a short composition tonight on the importance of the Word of the Lord in Scripture. Something for our edification. From your remarks, I presume you are acquainted with Holy Scripture?"

"Oh yes, Miss Mann," she said eagerly, "I have even memorized many passages, for 'blessed is he that readeth,' as Saint John says. There are so many wonderful passages that make the heart stop, such as 'And after these things I saw four angels standing on the four corners of the earth, holding the four winds of the earth . . . And I saw another angel ascending from the east, having the seal of the living God . . . to whom it was given to hurt the earth and the sea.' Oh yes, ma'am, I know Scripture, and it is truly *grand*. It reminds me of the Bard of Avon, whose works I have also memorized. But God sometimes seems very cruel to me in Scripture, He who 'hurts' the earth. And then my spirit fails in me, and I cannot believe."

Emily Dickinson's words that day — and every day thereafter — were quite a challenge to the other pupils. I could hear them take in their breath with little gasps while she confessed all this. She made them very uncomfortable. She made *me* uncomfortable. To explain the effect of it, let me just tell you that she was somebody who walked on the diagonal while everybody else was keeping to the square. You would see her at recreation, when the other girls were promenading happily in pairs along the walkways of the garden. Arm in arm they would be, bright and pert and gabby in their pinafores, gossiping about the menagerie that might come to Hadley or about some boy at home or about a bonnet. And then you would see Emily Dickinson, striking out solitary on the zigzag, disappearing into the woods to look for some anemone flower or decaying leaf. Well, she had one friend in her cousin Emily Norcross. But she worried the daylights out of *her* until Emily Norcross was asking to write home all the time to tell her mother to tell her sister, Mrs. Dickinson, what Emily was up to.

"Emily," I said soberly, "to speak of the words of William Shakespeare, many of them filthy and godless, in the same sentence with language inspired by the Holy Spirit is almost sinful. It is *impious*, you surely know. Now we will have no more from you today. Tomorrow, you will bring in your little piece and read it for us."

(I gather, Mr. Higginson, from some of your own

essays that you admire Shakespeare. But you must re-member that we were all under the spell of Miss Lyon and that 1847 was another age from the one we live in today.) Well, Emily Dickinson took my words well enough. She never *meant* to be disobedient. In fact, Jessie the cook often commented on how quick she was to help take away the plates at dinner or wash and polish the knives, which was her special task. Of course, often Cook had to swoop down on her from the kitchen because Emily might just be standing there in one of her trances, staring out the window at emptiness, or looking at her reflection in a knife. She was company to herself in a way I never encountered in any other pupil! Yes, she was just strange. I wonder, now, at my own foolishness in ordering her to write something and re-cite it before I had censored it. I was too inexperienced to see the danger.

Well, I asked the others (after I reprimanded Emily) whether they felt ready to stand up in Seminary Hall and repeat the holy formula: "I hereby give myself to God and will serve Him henceforth by shunning the world and its evil ways." I explained, of course, that one did not have to become a missionary or a school-mistress to shun the world. A woman could be mar-ried and might even wear colors and dance on occa-sion while shunning the world, in Miss Lyon's sense. It meant only loving Christ above all other people and preferring prayer to any other pleasure. Not hard, I should think!

It was heart-warming to me, Mr. Higginson, to find them all so ready to do this! Fanny Arms, a lovely plump blond girl with watery blue eyes, said her mind was always full of God and His mercies. Laetitia Snowe, from the old New England family who helped endow the Seminary, declared herself convinced from the age of two years that she was among the elect. Ever since then, she had conducted herself accordingly and worshipped the Lord as He deserved since He was the Fount and Image of herself. Malvina Stanton said she could think of no one all day long but Christ. Lena Aldritch, who later married the mayor of South Hadley, confessed that she prayed so much it was hard for her to find time for her studies. I could see that my task would not be difficult, at least with *these* pupils. And some, I must report, looked over at Emily Dickinson, staring into the fire, with reproachful eyes.

I thought it might have done her some good to be scorned and left alone that day, as she was. No one from our class would walk out with her. Still, that part of myself which I consider original, perhaps a little different from the herd, was sorry for her. Since I have always loved words and the life of thought, though within proper wholesome bounds, I pitied her. If only she could have been literary in the *right* way! I say this even now, with that book of her poems selling so well. I stood in the bookstore yesterday, crimson with shame, reading some of her lines. Oh pray forgive me once more, but I must ask you: How could you have allowed such a poem as the one on drunkenness, "I taste a liquor never brewed," to appear in print? Or the one called "Apotheosis," which begins "Come slowly, Eden"? Eden! What could she have known about Eden? Surely she cannot be referring to the sacred place of creation. She had no respect for the Bible at all, except as a source of violent imagery! Even a virtuous unmarried woman like my-self can construe from "Come slowly, Eden" only some experience of carnal delight! But *how* could she have had such an experience? She was all her life unmarried, living in that mansion of her father's and right under his eyes. You say yourself in your Preface that Emily Dickinson "literally spent years without setting her foot beyond his doorstep." Then *how* could she have written the ungoverned, even lascivious poems that she wrote? And she was my pupil. Oh, I am troubled, Mr. Higginson, deeply troubled.

I fear I cannot go on with this letter as I planned.

If you could find it in your heart to pity a woman like myself with little in her life but her memories, and many of those bleak, will you send words of comfort to me?

You see, I tried to put a stop to Emily Dickinson. She was under my hand as a child and I tried to put a stop to her: that is, to her frivolous (if not corrupt) imaginings, to her writing such ridiculously passionate poems, even to her continuance at Miss Lyon's Seminary. I accused her of things. I was her scourge and her inquisitor. Now I am afraid that I did her more damage than I knew. I am afraid that my persecutions helped her to *become* the blasphemous personage I thought long ago that she was. If you could write to me once more, and relieve my mind by assuring me of one thing — that she was indeed at the end *saved!* As a minister, you will comprehend the value I place on that word.

Please help a soul in torment!

> Very truly and respectfully yours,
> *Margaret Mann*

*M*y dear Emily,

Here is the epistle you asked for.

I would write to you more often, Emily, but your letters are so thoughtful I fear my own cannot come up to them. I am so occupied here at school. It is hard for me to answer. I do take time, however, to read your words. They always seem to fly, so that whenever one of your missives arrives, I sit myself down to study it and try to grasp its meaning. I note that in the letter before your last, you observe, "Did you ever know that a flower, once withered and freshened again, became an immortal flower — that is, that it rises again?" But Emily, the only Resurrection I know is the Lord's and so such ideas as these perplex and worry me. Especially when you add "Resurrections here are sweeter, it may be, than the longer and lasting one." "Here"? Do you mean on this earth? I think you do. By "Resurrections," are you alluding to the return of Spring? You are so bold in your expressions! You know how your excessive nature-worship annoyed our teachers at Amherst Academy and it is certain to anger Miss Mary Lyon, I do believe! Oh, dear Emily, do *alter!*

Have you thought how famous for her piety Miss Lyon is?

Here at Feeding Hills all is most comfortable, if taxing. I have come back from the holiday with many new dresses and hope to have occasion to don them and seem pleasant, at least to my own fancy! I have many friends here. Do you find friends at Miss Mary Lyon's?

Yours sincerely,
Abiah Palmer Root

*M*y dear Miss Mann,

I read your last letter with the deepest interest. I mean to reply to it at the length and with the care it richly merits. Alas, that intention cannot be fulfilled today! Once again my publisher has exacted of me many tasks and there is, in addition, a sermon I must write and deliver in Boston on the weekend. So I must briefly delay my reply and do beg your forgiveness. I found it wonderful — if occasionally rather sad! — to be supplied with so many details about my good friend's life in that school.

I do urge you to believe, however, that she was *entirely* good! Immediately to answer your anguished question — and without reservation in so doing — let me say that I am convinced as to the following: if anyone on this earth will be saved, Emily Dickinson will be, has been, *is.*

I knew her for more than twenty years. Hers was the most unselfish of dispositions, the tenderest of hearts toward the sick and unlucky. She was without personal vanity. It is true that in her last years she was no longer a church-goer. But, if you will read a wide selection of her poems (rather than only the one or two somewhat eccentric ones you mention), you will see that Nature itself was her church in which she worshipped the Lord most faithfully.

I can hardly suppose that you ever did her any damage, dear Miss Mann. For I thought my sorely missed friend Emily Dickinson quite perfect in every way. So I would not worry on her account. How I envy you your acquaintance with her as a child, when that great soul was, in the words of her revered Wordsworth, "holding Wonder like a cup"!

Yours faithfully,
T. W. Higginson

$\mathcal{D}$ear Absent One,

It is a cold dark day, so I must really be at Mount Holyoke Seminary indeed! This is so *plain* a place, there is almost nothing to wonder at, except the Absence of wonder itself! (Though I go into the woods when I can bear no more; and there I find nooks for the daisy and the columbine when Spring comes. Perhaps then, I can be happy. Yes, of course I meant Spring is a Resurrection! That is a metaphor, Abiah. Don't be afraid of it, it won't bite!)

I am reasonably contented, here, or try to be. I share a bed-chamber with my Cousin Emily, who is a Senior. She is an excellent girl, very pious like yourself, and she is kind to me, though we are very different. The teachers pretend to be cordial; but they do *watch* us, I fear, with the assiduity of the wolf, peering at his prey. It is not blithe, friendly, and comfortable here as at dear old Amherst Academy. There is no one like Miss Woodbridge of the witching eyes. I miss *you*, Abiah, more than I can divulge! (This is a new word I learned today; I am ever at my lexicon when it is possible. There is a *kingdom* of words, Abiah. Of it, I would one day be a Queen!)

I will tell you my order of the time of day. You will perceive that there is no room, here, for shirking. No time for dreaming and limited time for loving. Marriage is strictly forbidden to the teachers, I have heard, as is writing letters to beaux, or interviewing the same on Seminary grounds. Indeed, dearest Abiah, I do not think our martial English teacher, Miss Mann — a sobering presence, indeed — would be pleased that I sit here at my window, writing to *you*. She has taken a keen dislike to me, Abiah, I cannot tell why.

But here is my schedule. At six o'clock in the astonishing cold, I rise. I must say prayers to the "Eclipse," as I regard him: that dread and fickle Jehovah everyone so earnestly admires. (I still don't forgive Him because He wouldn't let Moses into the Promised Land and because He terrified poor Abraham, asking him to kill his only son! Was that kind? Was that compassionate? When I pray, *if* I pray, I pray to the Son, not the Father. I pray to Jesus, who was so tender with the Good Thief. That is what *I* do, Abiah, for that is how I see things.) Then at seven, we have breakfast in the great dining room. It is a chill, severe room; and I miss my gold primroses, Vinnie, Mother, and Father dispensing the toast and jam or pouring good hot coffee while the leaves fall outside or the snow veils our house in a silver silence. (How do you like that phrase "silver silence"? I am interested just now in "s" sounds. They are called "sibilants.")

After breakfast at home, and after I help with the washing-up, I am free to read or draw, though, as Father would say, "within suitable bounds for girls," which means for one hour or so before he feels I might lose my mind if it is not set right by baking bread! But here, after we tidy up, we go to devotion's in Seminary Hall and worship the "Eclipse" again. (Do not worry, Abiah, I shall not let them all know how perplexed I am about "declaring for Christ"; I am aware that that might be very dangerous for me. I suppose a hint of it *did* come out recently, when I could not tolerate a hymn sung in class. Yet I do not think my lapse was serious, or that Miss Mann was *really* alarmed by it, though she *has* made me write an essay as a sort of punishment. I hope it may make her approve of me. You know I cannot bear being ignored or, worse, despised!)

After Worship, I recite a Review of Ancient History. At eleven, I take a lesson in English composition and Milton from the aforesaid Miss Margaret Mann. Milton is a god, I can tell already; for, although we were forbidden to do so, I read all of *Paradise Lost* by candlelight as soon as the book was given us. Oh, it is *glorious*, Abiah, it is the moon and stars! At twelve, I practise calisthenics and then we have dinner and then I practice my piano or sing in Seminary Hall: hymns about the Missions, mostly. I would so much rather sing Ben Jonson's "Drink to me only with thine eyes." Methinks love songs beat hymns any day!

Then at three-thirty, I go to "Sections." This is where we give our Moral Accounts for the day. Absence (I am often "absent" of mind, thinking of you or Mattie or Sue), Tardiness, and a thousand other Delinquencies which I will not take time to mention. At four-thirty, we go to Seminary Hall, where Miss Lyon gives us advice in the form of a lecture. Unless we have a good and reasonable excuse for failure upon any of these items, they are recorded and A BLACK MARK stands against our names. The teachers say they mean to consult our happiness in everything they do. But their "happiness" already seems to me like Father's: a dark affair of Conquering Sin and Doing One's Duty. Oh, Abiah, I yearn to buffet the Sea of Pleasure, where there are poems on every wave and kisses in the curl of the foam. Now, does this scandalize you, my fair Maiden? Write to me!

Emily

Postscript: I do not understand, dear Abiah, your reluctance to appreciate the poems of Lord Byron. While he is, I admit, not devout; and although I would agree that the Sweet Singer of Hartford, Mrs. Lydia Sigourney, is certainly more circumspect, do you not find that your pulses beat more rapidly upon reading his dazzling Venetian love poems? Austin smuggled Byron's autobiographical poem called *Childe Harold* into my trunk before I left for the Sem. I read it each night by moonlight when Cousin Emily Norcross is asleep. He is a *poet*, Abiah. We cannot expect him to be as quiet and well behaved as a candlestick maker. Poets are wild in their hearts, you see, if not in their acts. Alas, I worry sometimes that I shall never make a poet. For what wildness can I do, shut up here?

Write to me!

𝒟ear Friend Emily,

That I do not write is no measure of my sentiments for yourself which continue unabated on the whole. I do wish you would discontinue your habit of scolding me for not writing.

Here at Miss Campbell's, the days are long and filled with labor as they are for yourself. I am learning French, cookery, embroidery, the elements of housekeeping, arithmetic, botany, and Scriptures. My roommate is a pleasant person from Northampton with very smart bonnets I always covet! Have you put your hair up in a roll or do you wear it still at the sides of your face?

It distresses me to hear you speak of avoiding the Church. There is no peace without yielding to God's demands of us. Dear Emily, do reflect and abandon your evil worldly ways of reading such poesie as you mentioned. I shall not repeat the name (my Father says it is infamous).

At the tea after meeting, when I visited my parents last Sunday, there was a very kind young gentleman who spoke to me. His name is Samuel and he will be entering Divinity School soon. Are there any young gentlemen who speak fondly with you?

Sincerely, your friend,
Abiah Palmer Root

*I*n the woods there is the last faint glimmer of light
before the dark shroud of Winter closes over.

In the woods there is a word

In the woods,
There is a word

In the woods, there
is a
Word

In the woods, there
is a
Word
that bears
a flowering name:
Crocus or Arbutus
or Death,
the last white bloom.

In the woods . . .

$\mathcal{D}$ear Mamma,

Yes, I suppose it might be enjoyable to accompany Emily home and have Thanksgiving feast with Uncle Edward and Aunt Emily.

If it is important to you, I will accept their invitation.

But you know I am always a little afraid of Uncle Edward. He tries to be affable, but he finds it so hard to smile! Then if I smile at *him*, I imagine myself guilty of an Impertinence. Aunt Emily is always most affectionate, but she can drive one half crazy, asking, "May I get you something? a sweet? a pillow for your back? another glass of grape juice? a shawl for the chill in the corridor?" and so on and so on, in her whimpering tones. You may recall that time you told me about when Cuz Emily lost patience with her ma and said to the guests, "Would you like to hear 'The Star-Spangled Banner'? Would you like me to recite George Washington's Farewell to His Troops? Shall I read aloud from the Declaration of Independence?" Her ma just plain exasperates Cuz Emily.

There are those here whom *she* exasperates.

How does Willie do, Mamma, and is there to be sledding this winter with our crowd?

Your loving grand-daughter,
Emily Norcross

$\mathcal{M}$r. Higginson:

Since I received your letter about my former pupil and your protégée Emily Dickinson, I have been in more spiritual anguish than before. Although you did not really reply to my own letter, especially to my question, How could you sponsor a poem about drunkenness?, it is clear to me that you *sanction* the life of Emily Dickinson! That you thought it a success, as well. That you approve, for example, of all these verses of hers that take on the subjects of life and death without expressing them as befits a Christian. Why, that one poem called "The Chariot" that starts out "Because I could not stop for Death" is just plain godless: Death coming for her like a spook in a carriage and the woman ending up not in Heaven but under some mound in the earth, as if there were no "I am the Resurrection and the Life," and all the rest of it. I taught her for a year, only, but she learned nothing from me; and, worse, she learned nothing from Miss Lyon.

Please, Mr. Higginson, help me to think of her as you do! Or else, let me attempt to make you think of her as I do!

I must go back to what I was telling you. (Yes, I know you are busy, you are an important man! And do you know, I do not care overmuch? The old become very vicious, very tenacious; and so am I becoming!)

There was a meeting of the Missionary Society on

October the first, the day before Emily Dickinson was to turn in that penitential essay I made her write. The Missionaries — they still exist, the school has never changed — are young ladies who intend upon graduation to labor for the conversion of the heathen in far-off lands. Miss Lyon was sometimes successful in joining each girl with a minister spouse; indeed, the marriages for which she was responsible were many. Sometimes she simply placed a pupil in the way of a partner who, though not a missionary, was nevertheless devout. Mr. Dickinson, Emily's father, was not yet a member of the Church in 1847; and I doubt he wanted Miss Lyon to find Emily a husband. On the contrary, he seemed (when I met him) intensely possessive of her. But for her to *conform:* he wouldn't have minded that! Rather, I think he might have liked it, had the conforming been to his principles. I still wonder why he selected our Seminary; he seemed so worldly a man. Perhaps because of President Hitchcock, who knew him, and promoted Miss Lyon's cause in Amherst.

Anyway, at the meeting, we sang one of my favorite hymns (the sort of hymn Emily Dickinson detested but then adapted in her puzzling verses). I came back to my room humming it:

> *What though the spicy breezes*
> *Blow soft o'er Ceylon's isle;*
> *Though every prospect pleases,*
> *And only man is vile . . .*

How clearly I could imagine one of those godless lands far from our blessed New England, where the flowers are brilliantly colored as tropical birds and the water-falls gush into dark pools of sensuous delight in which heathen women, naked to the waist, bathe and splash! Oh, the ugly beauty of it! I fell asleep, dreaming of Ceylon, longing to go there myself as a spiritual re-former. (That "Eden" your "friend" Emily Dickinson writes about seems like it; but *she* gives in to it!)

In the morning, after a good breakfast of oatmeal and currant jam — we always ate well at the Seminary — I went to take my first class. When I entered my classroom, *she* was seated there. Strange, but in memory I usually see that enigmatic smile of hers. Often I see her smile and then disappear around a corner, always alone (though she did find a few friends among the older girls after her Christmas exploits, and they were quite fond of her, I believe, at least until she subjected them to too much of her intensity). Now it was as a *seated* figure, after all, that Emily Dickinson presented herself to my eye day after day for almost a year. But still I always think of her as standing.

"Good morning, Emily." I bowed to her. Miss Lyon wanted us to be as amiable as possible with the pupils. Young girls are, you know, pathetically vulnerable and when they are fond of a teacher, the teacher can do anything she likes with them. I have known mistresses who bragged that they "play the girls just like violins." (It is a crude phrase. I am not sure I like it. There is too much suggestion of touching in it, I think; and any touching was strictly forbidden at the Seminary. But I suppose they mean to suggest their absolute power over their charges.) It is very useful to inspire affection, especially if one wishes to refine a girl's conduct and morals. One simply encourages the child's instinctive passion to belong to someone. In the absence of a parent and before she has a husband, a girl can become quite dependent on an older woman. Then she can be molded any way the woman wants. At Miss Lyon's, of course, we molded for the Resurrection and the Life: we built for Eternity.

"Good morning, Miss Mann," Emily Dickinson said in that high-pitched voice of hers which seemed to float and shimmer like the light in the trees. "I hope you are very well. Is this not a rapturously lovely day, like another state of existence?"

As you can see from this, she was exasperating! As extravagant as a glass of wine. Meanwhile, the other students were entering the room with scarcely concealed curiosity. What would this Dickinson girl read to them? You could see them thinking how different she was from her cousin Emily. For Emily Norcross was a dear sweet stout little thing who was famous for her piety. Emily Dickinson liked her very much and never objected to all her praying or even to her writing home about the fact that Emily D. did not! I have to say that Emily D. was very liberal when it came to other people's beliefs. So little shocked her. It was really a fault in her. In fact, I saw her talking one day to Molly Acrefield, who had once worked as a mill hand, asking her about the mills. Molly was a sly, fast one, she was. One of Miss Lyon's charity cases. Proud Squire Dickinson would never have approved.

I decided to get it over with immediately, so I said

very pleasantly, "I think now we'll ask Emily to read us her essay on 'The Importance of the Word of the Lord in Scripture.' Then we will go on to my opening lesson on *Paradise Lost*. Do come up, Emily."

I indicated the teacher's desk so that she might stand there and garner some authority. I did not want the exercise to appear to be mere punishment. Emily seemed to ripple toward the desk like a brook over a meadow, so fluent was her motion; so uncanny, always. She clutched several sheets of paper, but as I recall she scarcely looked at them. Everything she read sprang to her lips from within. I will tell you, since you may know how she wrote only from those poems in the book store, that her writing style as a girl wasn't crabbed and tight and stark at first. That is, if she wrote prose, she wrote in a sort of high-flown, ecstatic way. She even tried to punctuate correctly — more or less, for of course she liked dashes the way a cat likes cream. But now I look back, dashes must have seemed to her like links in the bright necklace of her feeling; for she *felt* like no girl I have ever taught. All that feeling welled up as she spoke; it was like a river or a sea and all the curt evidences of prosaic communication: dashes and commas and periods (all the things I was supposed to legislate) floated haplessly out on it. I have kept her essay these many years. Whenever I look at it, as I do now, I can hear her declaiming it.

"What is 'The Importance of the Word of the Lord in Scripture'?" she recited in her breathless voice. "My friend, Jacob Holt, has expressed it in a poem. He has written:

47

It is a fountain, full and free,
It is *the* book for you and me,
It will the soul's best anchor be,
Over life's tempestuous sea,
A guardian angel to the tomb,
A meteor in the world's dark gloom.

But indeed, although his words are very pretty —
and I wish I could write prettily like that, for when I
try, the words sometimes emerge jaggedly like pieces
of a sculpture I need to smoothe and fit together —
although he writes so sweetly, I do not think that
Jacob conveys the fire and fascination of the voice
of the Lord. Oh, listen to it in these passages: "And I
saw when the Lamb opened one of the seals, and
I heard, as it were the noise of thunder, one of the
four beasts saying, 'Come and see.' And I saw, and
behold a white horse: and he that sat on him had
a bow; and a crown was given unto him: and he
went forth conquering, and to conquer. . . . And the
Lamb opened the fourth seal, and I heard the voice
of the fourth beast say, 'Come and see.' And I
looked, and behold a pale horse: and his name that
sat on him was Death."

Perhaps the importance of the Lord's Word,
here, is that it sets us thinking about where we were,
even before Eden, and what will be our Last End —
that it gives us in these imperishable sounds called
"words" a diagram of the limits of the universe.
What is the "pale horse" but destiny and who is the
rider but the terrible bridegroom who comes for us
all? I think of him, sometimes, even when I am

eating apple Betty and spice cake or watching the trees blossom in the spring — I think of him! For, ever since my beloved Sophia Holland left this earth last year, I recognize that we go, all of us, to a marriage feast with Death. And then, I ask myself, Where will the *I*, the "me," of which I am so accustomed to think, be found?

How important is Scripture when it so fans our imagination and opens to us the rhythms of the stars and the tempers of the deep! How significant since the Holy Ghost — sometimes I think of Him as the holy spectre — who inspired the language of the Bible writes to us so well. My favorite biblical passage is from Matthew, chapter 6, and it begins at verse 28: "Consider the lilies of the field, how they grow; they toil not, neither do they spin; And yet I say unto you, That even Solomon in all his glory was not arrayed like one of these." *I say unto you:* it has the drama of the thunderstorm and the shriek of the eagle and yet it is as silken and tender as the skin of the day-lily herself when she first smiles up at the sun. The importance of the Lord's Word in Scripture lies in its consummate eloquence. It is an eloquence that one may everlastingly envy and admire. Before it, all who love words must be forever struck dumb.

Well, as you may imagine, I myself was struck dumb! When she finished, she looked over at me humbly and charmingly and altogether submiss; and I really think she expected to be praised. The other girls regarded her as if she had dropped from the moon.

"Am I to understand, Emily, that you think of the Bible as *literature?*"

"Yes, indeed, Miss Mann. The best that has ever been written."

"Is every girl in this class of that opinion?" I asked indignantly, looking round at them all as they sat blinking at us both. It was Julia Dame Bodfish, Miss Lyon's cousin, who spoke up immediately and as intelligently as she always spoke.

"It is surely *not* literature, ma'am. Literature is just flimflam. Except, of course" (here she caught herself up) "except for Milton, who was such a good man, or great sermons such as Mr. Edwards's, or Mr. Emerson's essays. I have nothing against books that improve you. But you cannot call the Bible anything but the *Bible!*"

The other girls all nodded their heads. Poor Emily got even paler than usual and her hand trembled. Again, I almost felt sorry for her.

"I want you to write fifty times tonight in your workbook, Emily, the following sentence: 'I will never call the Bible literature.' And I want you to pray fervently to be given the gift of faith. Your name has been tacked up outside the chapel door with the rest of the hopeless, and you know that Miss Lyon expects you at the special revival meeting this evening. Do not fail to appear."

"Alas, it will be useless," she murmured, "but I shall obey you in all things, my dear Miss Mann."

She always addressed me reverentially but as if we were the same age. Or even as if she were the older person. As I directed, she presented herself in Miss Lyon's rooms that evening — so pleasant Miss Lyon always made the prayer meetings for those without hope! They always had hot cider and doughnuts and prayers full of flowers and angelic hosts and harps. She saved the fire and brimstone for the believers, mostly. The other girls without hope were an uninteresting lot. You felt they had no minds to think with. They were just lazy fools and Miss Lyon pursued them because she was obliged to. But Emily was clever. She stood out. We needed to subdue that unruly spirit of hers; we wanted to make her submission an example for the others to follow.

Emily sat alone as usual, scarcely noticing the other delinquent girls. And as usual, Miss Lyon subjected her to open interrogation. "Emily," she demanded, "what is your favorite story from Scripture?" (Such questions were designed to reveal the pupil's temperaments, to discover how to appeal to them.) Emily thought a moment, and said roguishly, "Happy or sad?" When Miss Lyon said "Happy," probably expecting the birth in the manger or Christ among the little children, Emily replied that she loved the story of David, who made songs and who had slain the cruel giant Goliath. And that she was always pleased when she read about David loving Bathsheba, since a beautiful woman *should* be loved and Bathsheba's husband had neglected her.

Miss Lyon was simply scandalized by this and urged Emily to recall that King David had had Bathsheba's husband slain; that God had punished David as both an adulterer and a murderer; that the story of David and Bathsheba was one of violence and lust.

"Yes," Emily said vaguely, as if she were speaking from a far-off mountain-top, "love is a madness. Think of *Othello!* But they must have strongly experienced the glory of their passion for each other. How it must have burned in them in that hot desert country, where the breezes caress the face like kisses!"

Oh, we were in over our heads with her, I can tell you. And it got worse. I mean to relate to you everything that she did at Christmas. And then there was (as the coarser pupils called it) St. Valentine's Day and all she did then. I fancy it was on that day that I really came to see what she would become.

It is impossible for me to believe, dear Mr. Higginson, that you — not only a man of God but a man of the world, a Colonel of the Army — never perceived the *guile* of that young woman! Well, I can go no further until you explain how you came to publish such poems as I mention. I am aware that, as you say, she wrote harmless little things as well. But the corruption of the best is the worst, as the old proverb saith.

> Most sincerely and unhappily yours,
> *Margaret Mann*

I can't tell you, Austin, how much good your visit today did me! My spirits have wonderfully lightened! I have been very homesick, and with good cause, I think.

Before I explain, let me say that I wrote to you, Mother, and Father, that Miss Lyon feeds us all very well. And that is really very true. There is an abundance of food and it is served plainly but pleasingly. Last night, for example, we ate roast veal and applesauce and drank as much water as we liked! (Father would have to forego his claret here and I must do without my coffee; for any form of stimulant is strictly forbidden. But we may have juices if we want.) Nevertheless, it is very strange, but we are all very hungry. Hungry, in particular, for sweets. And so the cake — the gingerbread — the pie — and the delicious peaches you brought have all been completely devoured. We sat on our beds, Cousin Emily Norcross and I, and said a little secular prayer over every mouthful, urging it not to disappear. But when the last taste of chocolate left my lips, I knew the gates of Paradise had closed on me again.

Do not tell Father, he imagines all is perfectly proper here, but some of the girls steal baked goods and feast on them in secret. I have been told that there are fifty pies sequestered in bureau drawers throughout the dormitory! Although I have not done so yet, I feel the urge to thieve as much as anyone else. Perhaps more. My need is especially acute just after I leave the class of my English teacher, of whom I have become afraid. She stares at me, dear Austin, as if I were one of Dr. Hitchcock's specimens. Your older sister, usually viewed in the family circle as unremarkable, has earned a reputation with Miss Margaret Mann as a scoffer and ingrate. An ingrate with respect to serving the Lord of the Puritans and a scoffer with respect to the laws of English verse! The last, because I observed that, although beautiful, Milton's poetic style is not the only style in which one might write.

"What can you know of it, Emily," said she, "a girl of seventeen?" I do not think she realizes, dear Brother Pegasus, how much you and I read at home when Father is not watching! I doubt that Miss Mann has touched the hand of that foreign lady, Mrs. Browning, as I have in my heart, or been moved by her brilliancy. Pray never mention it to Father, I could not bear to wound or worry him, but I am already punished, Austin, for speaking of the Scriptures as works of the pen! My hand aches from the copying exercise I was set as a penance.

Now, Milton may be a god; but I am a poet, too, Austin. You must not laugh at me, dear Brother Pegasus, for I know you think of yourself as the only poet at home! But I have a Guardian Angel of Art, a young girl who looks just like me and sometimes a little like Vinnie's friend Sue Gilbert; and sometimes she has red hair like mine but sometimes her hair is black as Susie's. And she don't countenance blank verse. What *she* wants are sprightly lines full of sinuous fire, elfin lines like an adorable woman peeping out from behind a screen as she dresses, or terrible angry lines like a thunder-clap in the sky. Well, you will think me foolish, Austin, if I run on like this — and pray don't tell Father that Emily fancies herself a poet. You know how he hates those "twiddle pates," how he excoriates Lord Byron, and how he thinks "scribbling ladies" like Madame de Staël will never come to be redeemed by marrying!

How I long to come home, Austin, even if only for Thanksgiving! Thanksgiving is the sole holiday on the calendar not frowned upon by Miss Lyon, I suppose because she so esteems William Bradford of Plymouth Colony. She has given Emily Norcross and me permission to spend the holiday with you. So do not fail to come for us — come early, Austin, I long for the moderated freedom of my own dear home!

You will, I hope, note the decorous appearance of this letter, penned almost entirely without that stitch of intellection, the dash, now forbidden to me! What fibbers the teachers are, though. Miss Mann uses dashes herself.

Your affectionate sister,
Emily E. Dickinson

I am at the window, as always. Before me are the hills, wreathed in a darkness so full of strange hidden light it seems to speak to me both of the past and of the future. Over the hills lie my room at home — my writing table, my basket of pens. Do you know that I see them in dreams, ever since you first spoke to me? I remember how you entered my chamber, so soundlessly, and the garb you wore — all white — and the way you looked at me and the way you *talked!*

You seemed to know that I was lonely. And *how lonely!* You knew that I have always been a Mourner among the children; that when alone, I grieve; that I need and that my need is very great. I closed the chamber door and we conversed together. Do you see, I felt that you were drawn to me — that, perhaps, you could love me, and that, if you did, I would come to learn the very Secret of life itself.

Then Father intervened and I was sent here.

But you came to me in the night that once! And I thought you said you would return. Oh, come to me again, like a Spirit of the Air!

All the others I love are mere Phantoms of your grace.

Come to me!

$\mathcal{D}$ear Sue, dear Departed One,

I have been writing at my window, gazing by the candle's flickering stare at the diminishing shapes of the hills out yonder. And then I thought of you, and our happy times in Amherst this past, long, lingering gold Summer when the fairy folk were in the grasses and the starlight long in coming, bright, upon the horizon! Do you think of me?

Are you still devout, dear Sue? I feel I have not yet made my peace with God, He does not seem to be the One I crave. I am still a stranger to the delightful emotions that fill the hearts of those around me, who worship so smilingly, as my teachers say.

My studies at Mount Holyoke Seminary are rich with Challenge; but the courts of the godly here are not often populated with artists. I take drawing lessons but humor is not allowed, so those little caricatures I enjoy making (they made you chortle) are forbidden me. Do you still try to write golden verses? Do you know, I sometimes fancy I could be a marvelous poetess, should Someone take an interest in what I do. I am very *alone* here.

Be my good angel! And from your bright place among God's favored, do write to me, Sue!

Emily

I have been hungry, many years,
My appetite, my pain;
I have shed famished, angry tears,
My suffering, my gain.

I have been Hungry!
Heaven will be like this:
To dine on . . .

Hunger is the twin of Love.
You feed it and it grows.

I had been hungry, all the Years.
My Sustenance had come.
You and not God, my food . . .

I had been hungry, all the Years —
My Noon had Come — to dine —

I had known Hunger . . .

$\mathcal{D}$ear Emily,

Thank you for that brilliant letter full of winged words and starry expressions! How remarkable to think that I am acquainted with someone who writes as effectively as yourself! You must be quite proud of that talent of yours. Certainly I should be, were it my own. Ever since your sister, Lavinia, had the insight to bring us together in friendly association, I have been much impressed by your gift for language. A number of your letters lie about, which I have been too busy to answer. But I will say that a letter from you often fills me with rapture, and there is precious little in my day that does.

I continue at your former Academy here in dull old Amherst — though you love this wretched, doddering town, I never shall! — and when school is done each day I return to my brother-in-law's house to be a maid-of-all-work besides. Mr. Cutler knows I must be very industrious about my studies if ever I am to earn a Teacher's Certificate. Should I be apt to forget it, *not a week passes* without a missive from Brother Dwight reminding me of the fact.

I do not think, dear Emily, that you and Lavinia, so fortunate in your wealthy connections, in your loving parents and generous brother, could possibly imagine how dreary life can be in my circumstances. Dwight tells me that as soon as ever I am eighteen, lessons must be over for me and lessons must begin for others; that is, that I must go out as a Governess. How I do envy you, dear Emily, even though I realize how wicked I am to do so! For you will only grow and develop in the coming years as a creature of intellect and sensibility. (Indeed, perhaps one day you will be the Great Poetess we spoke of that lively afternoon in your parlor, when you quite dazzled me, as I guess you wished to do, with a few of your verses.) I, on the other hand, am destined to become even more of a drudge than I am at present.

To illustrate what I mean about drudgery, let me record that while you have a few well-polished knives to collect each night after supper at Miss Lyon's, I must scour the pots, lay the fires for the morning, bathe the children and put them to bed; and all this before sitting down to my lessons for the morrow. You may imagine that, although I too have literary ambitions, not much of any value can be composed under conditions such as these. So, although you are able to write to me at will, seated as you say by your open window (do you not fear a resumption of those tiresome colds of yours?), I must fight for a few moments, not to compose poetry, but merely to complete the lessons that will liberate me at last from this Prison of Dependency. And while, doubtless, *you* will be encouraged to express and develop yourself by your Pen in years to come (I do not anticipate your Father's forbidding it; he is all bark and no bite, I think) I shall be instructing spoiled darlings in sewing and deportment until I am old and withered and no longer "embarked upon Boundlessness" — or however you so extravagantly put it last summer!

Well, I am quite out of sorts today. So out of sorts, I might be willing to marry, even, to escape housework.

But then, of course, I should have to marry a wealthy man! And Squire Dickinson is already claimed!

On a happier note, I am reading in secret, by candle-light, Alfred Lord Tennyson's *Poems*. One is called "The Lady of Shalott," about a girl in King Arthur's day who weaves beautiful cloth alone in a tower until she falls in love with Sir Lancelot du Lac. She dies when she stops weaving in order to gaze at him! We have often talked about how marriage may spoil a female artist's life (or, indeed, any woman's life!). Do you think Lord Tennyson had that in mind? But, as I say, I shall be forced to marry, to find someone to burden himself with me; or else die, an old crone laboring for her livelihood.

Alas, this is not a cheerful letter. I wonder you bother with a person who composes such self-absorbed letters as the ones I send to you. I find it so hard to hide my moods. And Death has me in his bitter grip today because I "watched" last evening over the final hours of Mrs. Addie Moultrie. Oh, Emily, it was a harsh experience! There really *is* a "death rattle," a sound that starts in the bottom of the throat and gets louder and louder like a rat screaming to get out of a hole. Then there comes the most terrible smell from the sheets of the departed. I had to help clean the body, for it had soiled itself. I will never "watch" again, no matter how earnestly I am implored. Be grateful, dear Emily, for your happy and untroubled days at Miss Lyon's. If you knew about Death, you would make each instant you are alive more precious to you.

Yours,
Susan Huntington Gilbert

Postscript: No, I shall not be in Amherst at Thanksgiving. Yes, it would have been most agreeable to see you then; but I shall be visiting with my other sister. A welcome relief from Brother-in-law Cutler's.

Goodbye,
Sue

I write to you, Susie, sitting at my little desk by the window. But *this* window is, blessedly, at home! The street is still dark as the bottom of our well, and only a single star poises itself like an asterisk over the steeple of the church. I think you could become my single Star, dear Susie, and my dearest Friend. My heart yearns to relieve yours of its misfortunes — I do apologize for begging letters of you when you are weary. A letter is such food and drink to me, and I am ever *hungry.*

The event you describe, watching at Mrs. Moultrie's "journey over," fascinated me! To observe the Soul as it waits for the King to enter the room: this would be an experience most valuable to anyone who *thinks!* But I grieve that it pained you and I trust that Mrs. Moultrie is now happy in a better place. I wonder how you do today on your holiday in Geneva and say my thanks for your affection with each breath that I draw! But could you not write to me more often, Susie? I have had only that brief, appetizing letter from you since September while, although Miss Lyon leaves us little time for letter-writing (whatever *you* may suppose), your Emily has sent to you twenty-two letters full of fond conversation. Ah, there I am, begging once again.

I *know,* or perhaps it would be more tactful to say I can *surmise,* how laborious life is for you just now. But some day, dear Susie, it will change, I *feel* it will; and indeed I find myself pondering each night what I might do to make your life happier. Could I share my own good fortune, as you describe it, with you, I should do so in a flash, in a trice, in an apocalypse of fond desire. Marriage is a parlous state indeed — but too bad *I* cannot marry you, Susie, and set you up, a satin eminence, in my Parlor and Heart! Now maybe you should think of marrying Austin — when he gets less rough and gruff and his locks are better cut — though I should be jealous if you do. I am the "man" for you, "Brother Emily" is my name!

I do not hear much from sweet Abiah. Indeed, the more I write to her, the less am I answered. My little circle of friends is diminishing; one after another prefers the call of some young swain. Could we not be constant to each other, Susie, and grow into a pair of decayed old ladies together at the end? Even when that dangerous Prince comes for each of us, shall we not be faithful and love each other more than *ever* we love him?

Father and Mother are not yet awake. The house is still as a sleeper in one of the marble houses out yonder in West Cemetery. This is my precious season: for writing you, for writing those verses I told you of, for stealing downstairs to try out a tune or two on my piano. They will surely go to Church today, which afflicts me, as I do not know how to escape going; but escape I must! I know you are religious, Susie, and will not understand my anger against that old burglar God, who has stolen away so many of the souls I have loved. You would do far better at Miss Lyon's than I.

But perhaps Father will let me off, since he worries so about my health. The rain fell in torrents as we made our way yesterday from South Hadley. The wind howled around the sides of the mountain over our heads, and myself shrank and shivered under the blanket Austin drew round me until at last, the spire of the Meeting House rose to my delighted vision, and soon we were at our door. Mother said as she took my soaking wrapper off, "Child, I shall *never* let you return to that dismal place if you cannot look less pale and chill," and indeed, dear Susie, I feel I am turning to stone at that venerable institution, so bleak has it come to seem to me!

My studies are not difficult; but I do not feel accepted or acceptable. Your vision of my pleasure at school is rather faulty, Sue. There is little Poetry there, only Prose. I hunger for merriment. Father always recites to Austin, *à propos* of what must be his career in business, "Man was made for action / Action's his sphere"; well, I am made for action! But the only "action" Miss Lyon envisions for any of us is life as a schoolmistress or a missionary — and with my deficiencies, I am scarcely suited to that! — or as a wife. And, as you know, I sometimes think I could more easily be a ghost than a wife, so *eradicated* do they seem (if Mother is any example) by those lords of life, Men!

There is one beneficent aspect of Miss Lyon's training, though, I think, and that is that she hates what she calls "gentility," and "genteel nothingness" for women. She finds women capable of true learning. So we are set at Austin-subjects: Latin, German, calculus! Father is amazed but rather pleased by it (though he tells me not to get grand ideas, for even brilliant women must not hope for perfection in study). But I am at present engrossed in the chemical study of oil paints. The colors absorb me more than the ingredients. I am scolded, here, for what they call "worshipping trivial beauties." Well, then I shall have to be scolded. Let Beauty haunt me till I die! What I should *like* to do is draw the flowers they have us pluck from the woods for Botany. We press them, but it is not enough. I mean to draw them, then, in words. Would you like to see my "drawings"? I shall send you a short Anemone when Spring comes: each syllable will be a petal.

I have one real Nemesis at the Seminary, my English mistress. How tragic, since you know how I love to write compositions and how completely I yield myself up to the music and sway of words on the page! But everything I write for her, she thinks "extravagant," "improper" so that I have begun to be afraid of her. She thinks of me as an Insect among the roses. But I am a Bee, not an insect, and an industrious one. How industrious, the Ages will reveal. Write to me, Susie, I depend on you. You are my Avalanche of Sun.

Your friend and admirer,
Emily Elizabeth Dickinson

*N*otice to Miss Mann concerning
Miss Emily Dickinson, Junior School:

Like everyone else under my direction, I regard Emily
Elizabeth Dickinson, who came to us well recom-
mended by President Hitchcock and her teachers at
Amherst Academy, as a "Candidate for Eternity." I
don't think anyone can imagine how it has always
weighed on my heart: the fact that my real task as a
Principal here is to direct souls to Christ.

Therefore, what you told me yesterday, Thanksgiving Day, about Emily's behavior, both in and out of
the classroom, worries me exceedingly. That she seems
to be rather original in her use of the English language, I cannot but applaud. I want my girls to think
for themselves — within limits, of course. What you
report about her fondness for Webster's lexicon and for
learning the meaning of unusual words, I do not find
odd. On the contrary, I find it praiseworthy! Nor am I
worried by her intensity. All the Dickinsons have temper and flair. Remember their auburn hair. It is a natural characteristic in such folk. And I have observed her,
far out in the fields alone. Clearly she has a passion for
nature. Mr. Emerson would distinctly approve.

However, your other revelations — about her continued indifference to the whole problem of Salvation
and joining the Christian Church, as well as the star-

tling dilemma of her indecorum in the classroom (speaking of Scripture in the same context with indecent plays, etcetera) — are more worrisome than I can say. I would not feel that I had done my duty toward her dignified father, who seems the very soul of Honor, if I permitted such tastes to flourish in his daughter. Well, we will drive them out, like Satan from the Garden!

But we must proceed with all manner of Conversion cautiously, since her health is not robust. I allowed her to return to Amherst for Thanksgiving for that reason, though even before you wrote to me I had had an inkling of her unconformity and was minded to keep her here in a further effort to stamp it out.

We must pray and watch, Miss Mann, watch and pray. She is still very young. I cannot believe that she will resist joining the rest of her schoolmates ere long! You might use her fondness for language as an enticement. Pray reflect upon it!

Failing all else, we can deny her her Piano lessons, which she loves.

Her Salvation is more important than social accomplishments.

Mary Lyon
Headmistress

*D*ear Miss Mann,

I am distressed to suppose that any letter I might have sent to you would cause you such pain as you describe. Moreover, I am chagrined that you attribute to me some moral blindness with respect to my late dear friend, Emily Dickinson — a blindness that you seem to think is responsible for my published support of the first printing of her poems one year ago.

I do not think you knew Miss Dickinson in later life. So innocent was her demeanor, so like a child's in fact, that when I first visited her home in the 1870s and heard the light patter of her step in the entryway of the parlor, where I waited, I imagined that some young niece or nephew was preceding her to greet me. Because of the vigor and toughness of some of the poetry she used to send me, I was expecting a stern person, ferociously self-possessed. But she was gentle and receptive beyond one's most delicate imaginings, shy and ethereal and like one of her poems you *would* appreciate about rare field flowers.

I remember how we talked that afternoon. Or rather, *she* talked, almost incessantly, as if she had not spoken at length to any human being in some time. I took the measure of her life that day. I met her forbidding, tight-lipped old father. I observed the solemn house with its sole source of light, it seemed, her conservatory — her white jasmine flowers lighting the ubiquitous dusk! I remember her speaking with frank delight of her own chamber: "A turn of the key in the lock, and I have my liberty!" The married brother, living across the way, did not seem very interested in her needs. (I learned that, after her parents died, Miss Emily — with no money of her own, no inheritance — had to ask him for everything, even her clothes. He was kind enough to her, but he was a tortured man.) The sister, Lavinia, was, and is, a well-meaning but somewhat dotty lady who habitually cherishes over two dozen cats. Miss Emily was by then a recluse; but it was she who did the honors of the house when it came to funeral cards or wedding salutations. She was not averse to the world, or to the people in it. But she had an inner world, I fully realize now, to cultivate.

Your objection to such poems of hers as "Because I could not stop for Death" is understandable, I suppose. Emily Dickinson's was an original mind that disdained the commonplace. That being so, she was sometimes led into rather gothic forms of expression.

But I cannot emphasize too strongly my belief that she was a most virtuous lady. Indeed, Mrs. Mabel Loomis Todd's observations in "Bright Bits from Bright Books," which you may have read recently in the *Home Magazine*, declares that Miss Dickinson retired from the world because of her impatience with the insincerity of social forms. I myself think that judgment not unlikely.

If you do write to me again about her life at Mary Lyon's, Miss Mann, please know that I shall receive your letters primarily out of affection for my late friend and in loving curiosity about that part of her life I did not share. Of course, I do, as a minister, wish also to comfort you. But do be assured that my opinion of Miss Emily Dickinson can never be altered.

Sincerely yours,
T. W. Higginson

$\mathcal{O}$ur Autumn Guest is crimson —
A minstrel, sere but gay —

The Guest is brilliant crimson —
A dream in Bright array —
A Leafy dream

The Guest is gold
and Crimson —
A Leafy Guest
in Bright Array —
Usurper of the Summer,
Ah! Stay —

So, be the Distance far
From her sweet Heart to mine,
So, be the Music close
'Tween her far Words and mine.

So, though my Suit to her's
Not how she wants to sue,
So suit my Ways to hers,
That strange and subtle Sue.

*M*r. Higginson,

I am in receipt of yours of the thirtieth November.

Yes, I have read a number of explanatory essays seeking to excuse the poems of Emily Dickinson after they were published. Indeed, I could not escape your own "Preface" to her poems that prated of their "fastidiousness"! She did show a certain fastidiousness, even as a child, when it came to some things: I recall how clean she always was, her dresses immaculate, and her shoes brushed and polished. But she would write on anything: newspaper wrappers, the edges of her notebooks, scraps of brown paper, whenever she "heard something in her head," as she used to describe a line of verse. And, I insist, her *soul* was untidy! No one with so many flagrant and insubordinate carnal cravings can be called neat!

You say I will never change your opinion of her. Well, let me go on and try.

Miss Lyon used to say sorrowfully that Emily might not, simply, be among the Elect. I wonder how she would feel now, reading (as I did) that weird poem of Emily's that begins "Mine by the right of the white election"! Emily herself must have felt herself "elected"; but by whom and to what?

She returned to us from Thanksgiving holiday unimproved; still unwilling to declare for Jesus, still submitting essays of too independent a cast. But we could neither of us have supposed she would turn into a thief on the twenty-fifth of December or that it would be the daughter of fierce old Edward Dickinson who would be first to say the name "Santa Claus" — fat, bibulous emblem of secularism — at our Seminary!

You need to know that Miss Lyon did not believe in celebrating Christmas. She considered it a pagan festival, scarcely different from the Saturnalia. There were never mince puddings or punch or presents at Mount Holyoke. Nobody put holly on the door or swags of pine and certainly there was no kissing-mistletoe such as young people have now. Miss Lyon even forbade holly to grow anywhere near the Seminary and, if she saw a holly tree, creeping up in the shadow of some nobler bush, she always had it cut down and, as the words of Scripture put it, "thrown into the fire."

A week before Christmas of 1847, she decided that no girl could go home for the day. (I remember that Emily Dickinson was perfectly crushed by this and wept.) The twenty-fifth would be spent as a fast-day in order to combat the exceeding hardness and depravity of the human heart, a hardness that shows itself especially at what those worldly Episcopalians call "Yuletide." In addition, the girls were to be given exercises especially suited to correct one of their academic faults and one of their personal faults. The teachers had to decide which these might be. Mr. Pomeroy Belden of Amherst, one of the most energetic of the Revival preachers, was summoned to make an especially lengthy and sober sermon on the Eve of the day itself. And Miss Lyon was to hold a special meeting with the impenitent on the afternoon of the twenty-fifth in the Chemistry room. Girls who determined to attend, and, as she said, "give up their hearts to the influences of the Holy Spirit," were allowed to have tea and relax the fast.

We thought, therefore, that we had protected ourselves against the possibility of distraction or even of pagan merriment at that dangerous season. (It was becoming dangerous because, even in Boston, some of the Episcopalians had begun to hang wreaths on Faneuil Hall, and if a girl read the newspapers or the *North American Quarterly*, as I caught Emily Dickinson doing on a few occasions, she might discover that Christmas had grown into a festival there.) For some reason — youth, I suppose — our young ladies always seemed to nurse a craving for excitement, for "parties." I confess that by December, when the Seminary grounds were frozen and the sleet ripped and slashed at my face as I walked through the quadrangle to my classroom, what *I* longed for, even, was some physical comfort! It was painful to rise in the morning and confront the iced-over water in the washing bowl; it was hard to put your feet to the freezing pine floor. We had fires only in the dining rooms, classrooms, and recreation areas, but the sleeping rooms were no warmer than the air outdoors. When I looked out at the hills in December, it was always through veils of snow. Even Father and Mother had fires in the bedrooms at home, and how I missed them!

Maybe it was the cold that made the girls long for food so much. Their appetites in the winter, especially that winter of 1847 during the Revival, were simply formidable. Miss Lyon wanted nobody sick. There was far too much illness among the young in Massachusetts in those days. She was careful to give the girls plenty of cereal and fruit and poultry. She never stinted except on fast-days. So when Abigail Richmond suddenly died in our very midst a few days after that December twenty-fifth, I can assure you it was not from famine! Abigail was stricken with a strange malady known as "the Influenza." How it terrified us all to realize that Death had stalked her so skillfully and silently while we knew naught of it; and I can declare with complete confidence that his success at stealing her away so easily and unexpectedly led many hard-hearts to declare for Christ that very week! But, even though there were more fasts in 1847 than in other years, Abigail did not die for want of food. So the girls had no cause to do what they did, unless you would call Emily Dickinson's mischievous influence a cause.

Moreover, before you chastise Miss Lyon, even in your private mind, for what took place at Holyoke that December, remember that she was attempting only to form character and, with it, to build strong bodies. In self-denial, she herself always found strength, even joy. It was only natural for her to suppose that her beloved charges might do the same. Furthermore, she was convinced that the educated "new" women of the 1840s were less able to bear hunger, fatigue, exposure, and hard work than the women who bred up Miss Lyon herself. So she wanted them toughened; she could never tolerate silly women or frail ones. Indeed, I think what annoyed her about Emily Dickinson almost as much as Emily's failure to believe was her unnatural thinness and the fact that she always had colds. Squire

Dickinson claimed it was his daughter's frailty that caused him to take her home after less than a year. But we never believed it. Emily knew she didn't belong and so she gave up! Thus you may imagine my astonishment when I learned that by the middle of Emily's life she was wearing white, like Miss Lyon herself! Of course, Miss Lyon wore white because it is the color worn by those in *Revelations* who have passed through the valley of tribulation and are washed in the blood of the Lamb. Miss Lyon knew she had suffered greatly and that she was a Christian martyr in her way. But what can Emily Dickinson — she who was rich and never had to work and could spend the whole day writing poems as I myself could never do — what can *she* have suffered, I ask myself? Anyway, she evidently accepted some of Miss Lyon's teachings, we are forced to suppose — on the importance of self-control, for example — or how do you explain this little item? I've culled it for you from *Poems:*

> To fight aloud is very brave —
> But *gallanter,* I know,
> Who charge within the bosom,
> The Cavalry of woe —

Why, that is just what dear Miss Lyon thought, just what she tried to teach the pupils — that the most important struggle for a Christian was with the inner man, and that craven emotions like self-pity or "woe," as the poem calls it, must be put down. We must do our duty here on earth without repining. Miss Lyon also taught that the spirit could be perfectly satisfied and perfectly happy only in paradise. Some of Emily's poems, to give her her due, say things like that.

Well, I am driving far afield of my subject. Pray let me return to it.

So the twenty-fourth was to be a fast-day, and the young ladies were to be assigned exercises to correct one spiritual and one academic defect. I won't bore you with a long list of what was given other pupils to do, but tell you only what I judged right for Emily Dickinson. I was chosen above all her other teachers to decide in this matter, since Miss Lyon knew that I was taking notes on Emily. I had come to suspect her of plagiarism, though I could not be certain of it — and, of course, I am happy to say that I was proven wrong about her copying, though the case was not tried until the Spring. But still, Miss Lyon knew me to be deeply concerned about the girl and absorbed in my study of her. So I was the logical person to make judgments about her corrective exercises.

Well, I had noted for some time that, while Emily Dickinson was enormously proficient in her use of words, she was sometimes a poor speller. Even Malvina Stanton, the worst writer in my class, could spell more consistently than Emily. A word was like a person to her; it could assume different appearances. Sometimes, I thought, she could be writing Chinese rather than English, though she was careful about *meaning*. In fact, I remember how she loved to tell us about seeing a Writing Master of Chinese in Boston who translated her words into his own tongue: "My symbols became his symbols, and it was one glistening web of language!" (My stars, how dramatic she always was! It was excessive, a kind of self-advertisement as bad as any by some actress-person. It disgusted me! As a Quaker, I was disgusted!) So I decided to set her a spelling exercise, as thorough as I could devise. I arranged the words she consistently misspelled in rows and ordered her to copy the right spelling of the word a dozen times. I set her only twenty words, for I did not wish to be maliciously severe, but it was quite enough for one day, especially if she planned to attend the Reverend Mr. Belden's sermon that evening. I remember that one of the words was "pecuniary," which she liked to write as "picauniary"; the others, I can't recall, except that they were elementary. I think one of them was "really," which she stupidly wrote as "realy." I can still see her bending dutifully above her notebook, writing; and how she would look up from time to time to gaze out at the snowfall, whereupon her eyes — a deep, rich hazel color and truly memorable — would cloud and darken. Then I knew she was lost to us, walking outside the windowpane in her thoughts, knee-deep in drifts. She loved snow: "It is so silent, Miss Mann, and I love silence. It has a glamour, don't you think?"

For a spiritual corrective, I made her write Florence Vane's admirable little poem I had seen in a newspaper. It's a song now and it begins:

> "Are we almost there? are we almost there?"
> Said a dying girl, as she drew near home.

Its conclusion is exemplary. For it describes the young girl's deathbed scene, and says,

> For when the light of that eye was gone,
> And the quick pulse stopped
> *She was almost there.*

I hoped the thought of a young girl's death might frighten Emily Dickinson sufficiently so that she would go to the Revival meeting in Miss Lyon's rooms; for there were only thirty girls left without hope in the whole Seminary, only thirty who had not chosen Christ, and she was still one of them. But the poem so depressed her as to rob her of all energy. (What I had forgotten was that the grave had already claimed a childhood friend of hers.) She finished the orthography exercise by noon-time; but I did not allow her to rise for bread and water with the other girls (this collation was offered instead of dinner, usually taken at noon-day). Instead, so slowly was she working over her copy of the poem, pausing to study the snow again and several times to sigh, that I ordered her to remain behind and finish. So of course she had not eaten even a crust of bread when she did what she did, and that might excuse her to some people, though not to me!

I remember that, when her sin was first revealed, Emily's class, together with the rest of the Seminary, was seated in the Hall. I had been delegated to read them certain improving but fanciful selections before Dr. Woodbridge came in to preach from the text "If any man lack wisdom, let him ask." Dr. Woodbridge's discourse was to be followed by Miss Lyon's sermon on the duty of giving ourselves up to the influence of the Holy Spirit; but Miss Lyon wisely felt that a little amusement (despite the fast-day) should be permitted the girls between their religious exercises. So, I was chosen to furnish it by reading a sweet poem culled from a magazine. In my opinion, it is better than anything Emily Dickinson ever wrote! It began:

One day, the lovely rose said to the Nightingale,
     Dear one! O stay!
Think on my lonely fate — I linger in this dale,
     Thou goest away.

See how I droop — my cheek grows pale with
     constant anguish,
          Longing for thee,
In vain the showers kiss my pallid brow —
     I shall languish,
          Longing for thee.

That charming poem, called "The Rose and the Nightingale," was the sort of thing we encouraged our girls to write. I gave it to Emily to imitate, whereupon she produced some bizarre lines about fleshless lovers meeting in another life, and the woman — for I take it, the character who spoke was a woman — devouring the man in a gaze that endured for all eternity. I still recollect all too smartly how shocked I was! And this, after Miss Lyon had described to the girls in great detail just what Heaven would be like. Certainly there will be no room for amorousness there; no giving or taking — in marriage or otherwise!

Suddenly, as I was in the middle of my reading, Cook ran into the room — I had never seen her in that part of the house — with her hands still greasy from pulling goose fat for the next day's dinner and her apron strings fluttering at her neck, crying, "They're gone! They're taken!"

Cook was truly distraught and since I was the only preceptress present, she came straight to me in her boisterous way, and shouted into my face, "They're disappeared, all my good peach jam pies, my rice puddings, my boysenberry tarts meant for this Sunday's trustees' meeting, all of them gone, not a crumb or a trickle in the pans, and done like a thief in the night. Oh, your young ladies must be the guilty ones, Miss Mann, and how could they be so thieving?"

She turned to the girls, who seemed less startled than I thought they should be, and said, "How could you all have done this when you know supplies are short and poor dear Miss Lyon is on a budget that worries her sleepless every night?" (Cook was a confidante to Miss Lyon, having been Miss Lyon's nursemaid when she was only five and Cook had first gone out to service. So Cook knew about the loans President Hitchcock had arranged and how Miss Lyon had to ride out every Spring on horseback through the neighboring counties, asking for donations. We never had the money we should have had for food and so, in order to be generous with it, Miss Lyon had sometimes to beg. To lose so much costly pastry: oh, it would indeed be a hardship!)

"Does anyone here know who is responsible for this loss?" I asked severely.

There ensued a silence that was as eloquent as a thousand tongues speaking at once. No young lady was going to tell me.

"I may assume, then, that you know who is to blame and are concealing her identity?"

"Please, ma'am, could not the groundsmen have done it?" asked Nettie Coolidge, who had a lot of grit, as I remember, and was often spokeswoman for a group. She later took up the Suffrage under Miss Anthony, I heard tell.

"No," I said firmly, "they could not."

Silence. I looked meaningfully over at the mantel, above which hung the mottos of the Seminary, embroidered by one of the girls who stood before me: "Sweet Home" and "We Are a Band of Sisters." The embroiderer, a delicate girl who died not long after she left Miss Lyon's — she married at nineteen and perished the next year in childbirth — was called "Freelove Perkins." Her parents were Quakers, like myself; with us, "Freelove" is one of the nobler names, standing for unselfish charity. I could always get a truthful answer from Freelove.

"You will tell me, Miss Perkins, I think?"

Sadly, she looked back at me.

"We did all take the stuffs, ma'am, in a manner of speaking. There has been hoarding this whole month, ever since last First Day. It pains me to confess that I have two pieces of peach pie and a whole pile of macaroons in my dresser drawer. Jerusha Cowles is my roommate. She has four pieces of raisin cake. I don't know why we did it. We did it very slowly at first, planning to eat it all today, secretly, after our bread and water."

"But how did you manage to remove all those sweets from the dining table?" I asked, since eating between meals was strictly forbidden among us, as was any kind of underhand activity.

"In our pinafore pockets. We told ourselves that it would go to waste in any case since so many of the feebler girls were sent home to escape the influenza. I am sorry, Miss Mann."

We had not that many rules at Miss Lyon's, now I

look back, even though there were some wags who called it the "Convent of Saint Lyon's." There were the "Recorded Items," which were seriously enforced, and then the "Unrecorded Items," a little more lightly treated. Strictly forbidden were the Recorded Items: Absence from School Exercise, Tardiness in Retiring or Rising, Absence from Domestic Work, Communications of the First Kind (that is, unsupervised notes sent between girls), Communications of the Second Kind (uncensored letters sent to the outside world), Spending Time with Others Behind Closed Doors, and Sleeping Behind Closed Doors. Before she left us, Emily Dickinson had been guilty of both forms of communication and of spending time behind closed doors with another: a young woman, in fact, who visited her from another seminary, a brilliant-looking girl with dark hair. But I would not have suspected her of the last Recorded Item — Theft of Food — because to everything that was physical, she always seemed indifferent. So you may imagine my shock at what followed.

Enforcement at our Seminary was based on a rather elaborate system of self-reporting; so Freelove was behaving in strict obedience to Miss Lyon's rubric. But the girls were also expected to proclaim the infractions of others for the goodness of the others' souls. I was astonished when all over the room one voice after another rose, crying, "Ask Emily Dickinson."

"We did nothing today, Miss Mann, whatever we did earlier. But Emily bragged that she would show us what adventure was, what a feast is, and how sweeter far is forbidden fruit. She said she is really Eve, that she was

Eve in another life, so she understands hunger. She isn't at all afraid. She don't believe in your rules and she got Tom the houseboy to help her."

Laetitia was the prettiest young lady at Miss Lyon's. She was usually quite restrained and self-governed; but she spoke very angrily that day because she really hated Emily Dickinson, why I could not tell. Emily was plain, yet she was never envious of pretty girls and always kind to them. Perhaps because Laetitia was so conventional, Emily's wit and singularity annoyed her. My heart ached. Once accused, a young lady had to present herself to be judged. And her trial would not end with me, but with Miss Lyon.

"Call Emily Dickinson in to us," I told Laetitia. She flew from the hall like a comet. I imagined her triumphantly entering that cold room where Emily hunched over her unfinished exercise. I pictured Emily standing up, her limbs like two straight twigs, and that scarlet hair catching and holding the light of the fire. I heard her cough.

Then, the strangest thing! When Emily entered the room a great hush fell over all the girls and myself as well. Then I had a vision. First I saw her walking, in that spidery glide of hers, all shimmer and float. And then I imagined that her upright figure dissolved and I saw her seated on what appeared to be a throne, wearing a white dress, and a gold crown. And then *that* image disappeared and I saw her sitting up stiff, with a book next to her, and her hand clutching a flower and gazing out at me, just gazing with her eyes full of words.

"*What* have you been doing, Emily?" I said to her, as tartly as I could.

"Oh dear, Miss Mann, it was just mischief, just fun. Starving men attach undue significance to food, perhaps. We have all been famished here at the Banquet of Righteousness. Mine was just a prank. In my father's house, we always have much food. I do respect the religious undertaking of your noble institution, but people must have puddings! So Dickinson tried to find them some. I thought Cook would be amused, and would just make more."

"And where is all that food now, Emily?" I remember demanding.

"Oh well," she said quite merrily, "I nibbled a little of it like a greedy mouse, but the rest is under my bed and in my closet. We should have had quite a feast this evening, those of the girls who were willing to enter and feed on my sweetmeats. Of course, it is true that there are no strawberries such as those Imagination fashions from longing, and a berry consumed tastes far less delicious than a berry envisioned!"

She was just a show and a trial, she was.

We collected all the food, which had not been the least harmed — Emily did have a dainty, careful hand — and I took her to Miss Lyon's chambers. I guess Miss Lyon had heard enough about the worldliness of Squire and Mrs. Dickinson to be forbearing with their daughter. Mrs. Dickinson, some said, ordered her clothes from dressmakers who worked from French designs — I suppose that's worldly enough — and the Squire sat the best horse in the county. They did go to the Congregational Church, or at least Mrs. D. took her children. But there was a lot of secular ambition in that house. Anyway, maybe Miss Lyon was forbearing or maybe she wanted the Squire's annual donation: a whole thousand dollars, we heard, a small fortune. At any rate, she scolded Emily but she did not expel her as she had expelled other young ladies that year for doing less. With the exception of stealing out beyond the Seminary to meet strange men in the woods — an offense so dreadful it was unlisted, though it was spoken of — the theft of food is regarded as the worst of crimes. And Emily never took it seriously.

For that matter, she seemed to take very little seriously: only poetry and art and her own sentimental longings!

I watched Emily Dickinson all the rest of that week and especially on Christmas Day. She went to none of the Revival meetings in Miss Lyon's rooms. Instead, during recreation hours she walked out to the pine woods beyond the chapel, and — she told me — all the way to the foot of the river. It was cruelly cold and so I was worried, seeing that energetic but insubstantial body of hers toiling along in the snow and out of sight. That Christmas was the quietest I ever spent at Miss Lyon's; on the day itself, not a murmur in the halls. But after the prayer meeting Christmas night, Miss Lyon said to me gravely, "Margaret, there are very few here with a deep conviction of sin. I have failed thus far with the multitude, however they may deny it."

Yet Emily Norcross declared for Christ before the New Year; and that cheered Miss Lyon enormously. So much so that she sent Emily N. out on a sleigh ride — the preferred treat of all the students — with several of her friends, such as Katharina Cobleigh and Ella Swenarton. Of course, Emily D. was not allowed to go.

For she was not one of the elect.

I do believe that, Mr. Higginson. She was not! She was a law unto herself. God despises such proud people. Moreover, He condemns those who set human love above their love for Him! And that is precisely what she did all during the Spring of 1848 before her father took her home.

Yours pityingly,
Margaret Mann

*M*y Susie,

For I will call you "mine," a mine of wit and courage, a diamond mine in which you are yourself the Sole Diamond.

It is Christmas Day. The others are all at a Prayer Meeting conducted by forceful Miss Lyon. If it is like all her other meetings, it will be a joyless affair. At its heart will be what pretends to be duty, what seems to be virtue; but what I sometimes fancy is the passion to make all souls alike, to quell in the individual spirit every idiosyncrasy, every rapture! Do you, Susie, believe that Our Savior, who came with such tenderness to share the common life of men, really wants us to renounce everything that is beautiful in the Nature his Father made? Miss Lyon might not agree that she asks this since we *do* do botanical exercises (which means gathering some flowers) and we *are* allowed to sing and look at pictures. But each assignment has fear of Original Sin at its core, like the apple in the Garden. And everything has one purpose: to make us Calvinist Christians. To prove us the Puritan Elect.

I have elected another path, another way. I cannot precisely describe it, yet. But it is a way, like the Way and the Truth and the Light. And I know it means that I will suffer. I call it my White Election.

Anyway, Susie, I think of you, for I am especially lonely tonight when at home we would be decking the halls with the proverbial holly; when John or Henry or one of the other young swains would be coming through the snow to take us riding in their sleighs. Does your heart break, any, over one of them? Despite all the silky whiskers and gallant profiles, you seem stonier than anyone — or so you were last summer — toward the Idea of Sweet Romance. Marriage, you speak of merely as an escape from toil. Ah, be stony, Susie, to everyone but me!

Tell me if you like what I write now. It is this: I am thinking of us, seated in the parlor near the piano. I am remembering the moment when I took your hand and you did not take it from me. Do you recall that we read *Kavanagh* together, the passage about Alice Archer and Cecilia Vaughan, and that I read it to you aloud? You recall how it seemed to describe us! "They sat together in school; they walked together after school; they told each other their manifold secrets; they wrote long and impassioned letters to each other in the evening; in a word, they were in love with each other."

Is not that what we were last summer, Susie? And do you not remember kissing me so sweetly before we parted that evening when you left for Geneva? But now you write to me rarely and, although I know you are driven *hard* at Brother-in-law Cutler's, I need you, too.

I have been punished, today, for a little theft of food. Everyone steals cakes and cookies here, we are all so hungry for sweet things and for some indulgence shown to us. Yet the others, I admit, adhere much better than I to the Rule of Conformity.

Write to me, Susie, and tell me that you remember the summer and

Emily

$\mathcal{D}$ear Godmother,

I thank you for the fluted cap you sent to me for Christmas. (Though, of course, we do not have Christmas here, we are still pleased to be remembered.) I have been attending many Salvation meetings at Miss Lyon's over the late December season, as we call it. I hope she will continue to hold them in Spring, every Tuesday eve. She wished us to make it an object of prayer that the religion in our "family," as she calls the school, might be continued. She said the very essence of prayer is its continuance and without it prayer is nothing. The same she said is true with religion and it is this which marks it from other things. She spoke of Eternity as being unchangeable and asked why we should not be unchangeable in our preparation for Eternity.

You will be distressed to hear that Emily Dickinson appears no different. I hoped I might have good news to write with regard to her. She says she has no particular objection to becoming a Christian and she says she feels bad when she hears of one and another of her friends who are expressing a hope, but still she feels no real interest. I think Emily a most perplexing young person. In many ways, she is no different from the rest of us. She keeps her herbarium very carefully and neatly, for example, with the flowers pressed and labeled with a fine hand. Indeed, our botany instructor says she is a model of precision when it comes to knowing the names and features and necessary nutriments of all the flowers. But yesterday she said to me under her breath in the botany room, "He has the facts. But where is the phosphorescence of his learning?" I find snippets and snatches of things that she calls "verses" dropped about our room and on them are drawings of little boats and passengers with sentiments about "Exultation" being a sailing to Eternity. Miss Lyon's habitual use of the word "Eternity" does fascinate Emily; I think the idea of it intrigues her. She says that it may be a place of "extended consciousness"! But there is more to it than that. She seems obsessed by thoughts of the dead. Sometimes it fair frightens me to see how deep she goes into melancholy brooding if you speak to her of the after-life. I never saw such a girl for yearning. She misses Sophia Holland, still, and for goodness' sake, Sophia has been dead and gone these two years! Just nobody talks about Sophia any longer. The world must go on. Even Mr. Holland has relinquished his grieving and adopted a young girl to take Sophie's place. But Emily still misses and talks about her and, indeed, misses a young lady called "Sue" from Amherst Academy, whom she also raves upon without end. This "Sue" is alive; but to hear Emily rattle on, she and yet another young lady called Abiah Root might be lost to her forever.

Indeed, dear Godmother, Emily is simply too bound up in earthly matters and human attachments. Miss Lyon has addressed her on the subject.

Why she cannot just declare for Christ and escape the punishments to which she now is heir — for her delinquencies — and thus save everyone in our family from embarrassment, I cannot tell.

Strange to recall how dearly Aunt Emily, her ma,

loves Paris fashions and how normal she is, despite her rather tiresome old-fashioned courtesy. Cousin Emily claims she herself will be the "Belle of Amherst" some day soon, but I find that hard to imagine. Her appearance is marred by her odd long upper lip and that snub nose and the too pale white skin that freckles whenever she goes into the sun without head coverings. Then there is her hair. Pure carrot color. She calls it "auburn," but I call it red. Gentlemen prefer a belle with radiant sable locks, I think, or fair-haired like Lettie Snowe in our class. I am unhappy not to be more blond, but at least my locks, as you will soon see, have a lovely sheen since I am brightening them after I wash with a vinegar solution. An ad for the latter appeared in *The Springfield Republican* and I begged Mamma to allow me to send for some. There are a great many handsome girls in our class. Each looks forward to Saint Valentine's Day, when it is rumored that some of the new cards called "valentines" might be sent to us by the swains at colleges round about. Miss Lyon has heard of this, and forbids us to receive any such greetings. But perhaps Daring Affection will conquer Grim Prohibition in this regard!

I did not write, besides, that I am ashamed in our English class, because I am Emily Dickinson's cousin. There are many girls who envy her her verbal facility. Indeed, dear Godmother, she is a very Paragon with a lexicon: words tumble forth from her endlessly! But I cannot predict what she will say and it is often, very often, out of our mold. She knows the rules of grammar and will use them when she cares to; but often she simply flouts them altogether. She has an odd way of saying only half of what she means sometimes, too. She knows how to set points ("punctuate," they are beginning to call it here) but won't always do it correctly.

And now she has taken to quoting a wicked play of William Shakespeare's called "Antonie and Cleopatra." Miss Lyon often speaks of Cleopatra, whom she considers an "independent woman." But anything about Cleopatra's married life, Miss Lyon sees no reason to mention. Yet it is just the business of her married life and how she used it to "exercise Power" that Emily is interested in!

"Emilie," as she sometimes calls herself to seem more piquant, I guess!

Well, she is always kind to me. I do like her, some. But she isn't out in the open, like the other girls. A lot of what goes on in her is underground. It makes me uncomfortable.

I give her the wisest advice I can, and set a good example.

> Very respectfully, your goddaughter,
> *Emily Norcross*

*P*assion is the going
Of an island soul to sea,
Past the houses — past the headlands —
Into deep Eternity —

Passion is the going
Of a desperate Soul

Eternity is . . .

Sue is
Eternity . . .

$\mathcal{M}$y dear Miss Mann,

You are in my thoughts today, this sacred day of Our Savior's descent to earth when, with divine condescension, He came to share our lot and rescue us from the effects of Adam's wickedness. I wish you joy, dear Early Teacher of my friend Emily Dickinson, on this day and all others!

I have reflected upon what you last wrote to me — did you know that you wrote on Miss Dickinson's birthday? — and feel that you may have been led by those strict customs of the '40s to regard too seriously what was merely a childish prank. As a girl of seventeen, Miss Dickinson may well have stolen a few cakes; what of it? She spent much of her later life, I take it, baking and bestowing them. Her father would eat no dainties but hers, and to the village children she was a legend at her window, reeling gingerbread down to them with a loving smile.

It might help you to know what was said of Emily Dickinson by a few gentlemen who were well acquainted with her. Your worry (surprising to me! but apparently originating chiefly from your acquaintance with certain love poems of hers) appears to be that she was not virtuous in her personal conduct. I thought some recollections of a family friend, Mr. Joseph Lyman, told to me over years and written down by me, might help you to form a very different opinion.

"Emily Dickinson," he said, "was older than all of us young folk in mind and heart. Her letters were full of rare and delicate wise touches. But she was 'Platonic.' She never stood 'tranced in long embraces.' She was unnatural in that way. Morbid. She was more spiritual than earthly. But very brilliant."

Mr. Lyman himself was known to have been something of a "lady's man," as the expression goes, and his interest for a while lay in conquering the affections of Miss Lavinia. Frankly, I never liked him. And the word "morbid" was, I should think, not applicable to Emily Dickinson, who is known to have inspired and returned affection in a most distinguished barrister friend of her father's, Otis Lord of Salem, whom she nearly married. But, as you see, Mr. Lyman's impression of the young Emily Dickinson suggests unworldliness rather than carnality.

Her brother, Austin, told me that sometimes her deeply meditative nature (a favorite book was *The Imitation of Christ*) made her seem "too high up for the things of this world," although she was a devoted friend to many. I don't suppose you have heard that she has been called by some "The Nun of Amherst." It's scarcely the epithet for the person of doubtful moral character that you describe.

Well, Miss Mann, you will perceive that your letter continues to disturb me. Nevertheless, I would be eager to know anything more that you can tell me — of plain fact, that is — about my friend's school days.

> A very joyful Christmas to you and yours,
> *Thomas Wentworth Higginson*

$\mathcal{D}$ear Emily,

Each letter you send to me makes me increasingly aware of your talent for writing, a talent you seem very much to wish to reveal to me. Well, you have made your point. I see that you are rather gifted. Not all your effusions strike me as equally successful, however. The anemone poem you sent seems crude. Your ideas are briskly stated, but you do lack craft. Perhaps you should try reading even more than at present you do.

I myself, as I have told you, have an equal interest in words but no time to indulge it. At this very moment, I am expected in the scullery since this morning is Sister Harriet's baking day.

So my note to you must be brief.

I do not wish to turn away from one of those many kisses that you proffer to me in letters; but I confess to being somewhat embarrassed by so much sentiment, dear Emily. I do not at all recollect sitting on a piano stool and holding hands with you as you describe, if, indeed, that was what you said in your last epistle (unlike you, I don't keep letters).

And besides, I thought it was Abiah Root whom you loved.

Best wishes, as ever,
Susan H. Gilbert

*S*usie,

Why do you torture me, darling? There is none but you in my heart.

Why are you so cold to me in letters when you are so loving to me when we meet? Do you not recall saying only last summer that we would be dear friends, and never part? That we would grow old together, read and talk and companion each other every day, like Jane Eyre and Mr. Rochester? You said that you loved me as I love you — that when the world is cold and the storm sighs piteously, I would ever be sure of shelter in one warm heart!

Do you not remember the dear letter you wrote to me after our day in the garden alone? It came to me when all the world was still — Thank you for the love it bore me then, and for its golden thoughts, and feelings so like gems, I was sure I gathered them in whole baskets of pearls! I mourn this morning that I have no sweet sunset or sunrise to gild a page for you! All that I write to you from this place must be down, down in the terrestrial!

I take a realy great risk in writing to you, Susie, for Miss Lyon reserves the right to open all our mail, and since she don't permit what she calls "exclusive friendships" among the girls — we are all to be equal friends and have no "alliances" — she could punish me harshly. For this letter shows, I know, how exclusively I have cared for *you*, ever since Love first began, when we sat on the steps above the lilacs and spoke to each other of the past, the present, and life to come!

The Soul selects her own Society, dear Susie. I choose you! And that is because of your beauty, your mind bright as diamonds, your sweet forbearance in adversity, your clever wit — and your eyes, Susie, that gazed into mine with such sweet candor. Ah, do not be sharp with

Emily

Postscript: There is a daguerreotypist come to these parts to take our portraits. Miss Lyon says she will allow it because so many girls die without their parents having images of them. Father means for me to sit. I shall hate it, Susie, for you know I need my "veil," my privacy. I cannot stand being "inspected" by a neutral eye. But I want you to have a copy of my image and I want one of you, sweet Image of my idolatry!

Postscript two: If you will not be kinder in your letters to your separated friend, I shall have to break the Rule and jump ship and run to Amherst and demand of you kinder treatment, oh mistress of my heart!

$\mathcal{D}$ear Emily,

I must ask you not to write to me again like that.

My brother-in-law came in upon me as I was reading. It is his custom to frustrate and slight me in any way he can. So of course he swept the letter from my hand and perused it before I could make him feel my full displeasure.

Your persistent sentimentality might be very dangerous for us both. William fancied at first, seeing "Dickinson" on the superscription of the envelope, that the letter was from your brother Austin. He was momentarily *certain* of it when he read such lines as "ever since Love first began." Of course, when he realized the letter was from *you,* and you are known to be emotional — are you aware of that? did you know that Abiah Root is said to have stopped writing to you, Emily, because you frighten her? — he was no longer angry, just amused.

I *am* fond of you, dear Emily. You are all I should have liked to be: intelligent, with a rare gift of self-expression, and well educated in the style of wealthy women. Your piano-playing, your German, how I envy you both! Your indifference to possessions, so praiseworthy! (Though I wonder if you would be so indifferent did your father not have the grandest house in Amherst or had your grandfather not founded the College! I have often thought I, too, could be quite above all worldly desires if my house, like yours, had ancient portraits on the walls and if my mother went out in the evenings attired, like yours, in velvet and rubies. Alas, my dear mother is dead; and there was little enough money to bury her. Perhaps it is easy to prefer fields full of buttercups to fine drawing-rooms, as you once told me you do, when a person has known both, as you have.) Anyway, I am surprised and pleased to have so attracted your interest. But I fear I cannot reciprocate all the high-flown sentiment you express, and must ask you not to continue to embarrass me.

S. H. Gilbert

*M*y darling Sue! These are the thoughts I would write to you, were it not so late in the day that letter-writing is forbidden. I have not heard from you yet, although days have passed since my last letter to you.

I do not miss you, Susie — of course I do not miss you — I only sit and stare at nothing from my window, and know that all is gone. Without you, I only wonder what I am and who has made me so. Miss Lyon presses me to declare my love for Jesus Christ; but he is a mere shade to me. He is more real to *you*, Susie, and to Abiah and the rest than to me. I am failing the daily "test for Religion." I have not yet declared for Christ. And today, the English mistress, Miss Mann, informed me that I must have a conference with her and Miss Lyon on the subject of my writing. They have been treating me most suspiciously. Cousin Emily Norcross tells me that I am thought to be "proud and stiff-necked" in my conduct and my compositions. How this can be, I do not know. Indeed, Susie, I work so hard at my lessons! Ever before me is Carlyle's injunction — you know it, we spoke of it — "Produce! Produce! . . . Work while it is called To-day; for the Night cometh, wherein no man can work." To them, however, all I do is uncanny strange.

I would declare for Christ if I could feel his presence in my heart as you do, and Abiah does. What I feel in *my* heart is a speaking Silence that is holy enough. But hush! tell no one of it. I have heeded beautiful tempt-ers. The Angel of *my* Annunciation the Testament does not speak of. I never came to you in white. Therefore, you do not really know me yet, Sue.

I write verse every day, seated at the window so that I can glimpse the morning blossoming into flame. I feel guilty to miss you so much. But then,

> Auto da Fe — and Judgment —
> Are nothing to the Bee —
> His separation from His Rose
> To Him — sums Misery —

I am required to attend a General Salvation meeting this evening with others who have not yet declared. Of 324 young ladies, I am one of only three who are left. The others, it has been pointed out to me, are the feeblest scholars, from the least distinguished families in the Seminary. Cousin Emily is so ashamed of me that I have placated her by promising that if the language of the Belief Statement is vague enough, I shall try and assent to it.

But a Word realy begins to live when it is uttered. I will not speak falsely. Every day is mighty, its possibilities are endless. I have always felt that. To live may be Bliss or Despair, I do not know. Art may be the only Lie that God allows. You see, I do not doubt that there is a God. But I cannot say that He is my Only Good. There, the capitals are creeping in. I am scolded for those. How can God be my only good when there is

Emily

*D*ear Mamma,

I think Cousin Emily Dickinson may find herself in more difficulty than before with Miss Lyon. I write to prepare you, so that you can prepare Uncle Edward. But first I must tell you how things go here.

Many have felt so long and deeply about religion, they are almost sick; and some are mortally afraid of backsliding. One of the converts said to me yesterday, "Oh, I dread vacation, I fear to go out into the world." During meals, scarcely a word is spoken and many there are who cannot eat because of prayerful concern. The whole house has become as still as on the Sabbath; every footstep is light and every voice hushed. During recreation hours, going to different rooms, we see two or three conversing quietly together, one perhaps a Christian, the other an awakened sinner inquiring the way to Jesus.

Emily Dickinson continues just the same, even though Miss Lyon has called her to her rooms several times and Miss Mann has made her the object of intense concern. Emily is embroidering a sampler just now with a legend from Scripture; but it is apparent to all that only the appearance of this work is of interest to her. She labors over it very diligently and is apt with her needle, but I am afraid that she manifests in this as in so many of her efforts an attraction to what the world calls "beauty."

I have not told you, Mamma, about Miss Lyon's feelings in regard to such behavior or what the secularists call "art." I am put in mind of them by the appearance among us of the daguerreotype artist from Northampton, who, with Miss Lyon's permission, has been making pictures of some of the girls since last Tuesday. I shall not say whether or no your darling granddaughter has availed herself of his services; but I *will* say that he set up shop in the hotel adjoining the Sem, and Miss Lyon surprised us by declaring that — provided it did not interfere with our studies or prayers — we might go over and have our countenances recorded for posterity. You know how fashionable it is to do this now; so there have already been many "comers" to the daguerreotypist's premises. But before anyone went over (going over to the hotel is seen as entering the world, and Miss Lyon often prepares us for it), our beloved Headmistress spoke to us at length about all these productions of the human mind such as painting, literature, and music.

Miss Lyon is always so honest, Mamma, and never conceals from us the fact of the poverty that suddenly befell her at ten, so that she was forced to become self-educated. The great deprivation for her, she said, was not learning to sing, as she is very susceptible to the loveliness of choral music. "I have sometimes felt," she told us, "that I would have given six months of my time when I was under twenty, could I have enjoyed the privileges for learning vocal music that my pupils now enjoy." She is very eager for us to acquire the best habits of hymn-singing, and to that end we practice daily.

But she thinks literature is often very dangerous! She

approves of Grimshaw's *Etymology* and she is greatly interested in the origin of words. She makes us use our dictionaries all the time: so tiresome! (Emily D. is especially fond of doing this; she claims her lexicon has become her "companion." It is almost the only thing she is praised for here.) Yet Miss Lyon is ever eloquent about the wickedness of novels, excepting such as *Pilgrim's Progress;* and from poetry, she usually averts her face. She says novel-reading is dangerous because it stimulates a taste for untruths. Poetry, too, she finds a "selfish" absorption, unless it be devoted to the spread of the gospel or to committing a fact to memory. Indeed, I must sadly report, Mamma, that Emily D. was recently chastised after Miss Mann discovered a verse she wrote in imitation of Lord Byron. (You will not know, perhaps, that he is a scapegrace English versifier especially despised here.) Miss Mann also reported Emily's facetious remark about John Milton as a "florist" — which, in truth, Cuz Emily made, I think, only because of the lovely flowers he pictures in his Eden. She takes many bold liberties, Emily does. She has a sense of humor that is very full of mockery! You may imagine that Miss Lyon did not approve of such a comment because it sounds so disrespectful to Milton. She said — in front of the whole Sem — that it was sadly typical of Emily, who always cares for beauty of form when she should concern herself with the beauties of holiness. (Even if you assign Emily a holy text like Thomas à Kempis's *Imitation of Christ* — Miss Lyon admires this work because it teaches the virtues of silence and contemplation — what Emily will prate of is its eloquent style!)

Indeed, Mamma, it is a great hardship to be tied to Cuz Emily! I try to be kind to her, but I wish Fate had sent me an ordinary person to be my daily companion. Though Emily D. has never been anywhere but Amherst and Monson, she might have come from Peru for all she cares about New England ideas and principles. In fact she says she's "enchanted" by the sound of the word "Peru," and she is, she says, "enamored" of all southern places like Zanzibar and Santo Domingo — and *Italy!* which she calls "My blue Peninsula!" She dreams over her *Woodbridge's Geography* as if it were a fairy story. She says that when you "come from the frozen North," as we all do, happiness lies in warmth and "the Love-South." But when, I should like to know, did Uncle Edward ever take that girl to any of these poor, dirty foreign countries, where there are papists everywhere, and thieves, and fleas in people's beds? Yet he, *too* — pray pardon me — has remarkable notions of what one should visit. Do you know he told Emily "I want to have you see the Lunatic Hospital and other interesting places, should you go to Worcester soon"? If *she* is always thinking something startling, Uncle Edward may be the same. He will have her on his hands forever, no one will marry her, and then they can be startling together!

But about the daguerreotypes: Miss Lyon is especially censorious of painting or any making of images unless the maker's purpose is religious. She herself studied drawing and painting for a year, she said, with Miss Orra White, from whom she learned to depict vines (for Christ as the True Vine) and to decorate china. She don't mind drawing if it is botanical and we are all set to copying maple leaves till our fingers ache. But we are supposed to say to ourselves every moment as we draw, "God is the true Artist." (Emily D. objects to that wholeheartedly and says God may have made *her*, but *she* makes her drawings! And she does love to draw. When she makes her verses, she puts little designs in the margins of the page.) Miss Lyon is so fearful that we may become too intrigued by "voluptuous colors" or "overly dramatic designs" that the only pictures she has hung in the Sem are a series called *The Voyage of Life,* about the soul's eternal pilgrimage. Rocks and water and a palace in the sky, and angels and a man in a boat! Emily D. told me she gets ideas from them! She had much better be doing her algebra homework, as she is failing in algebra!

We were positively *amazed,* then, when Miss Lyon said she would allow some of us to be photographed. She said that to have a likeness of their children is a blessing to parents, especially in these days when measles, diphtheria, scarlet fever, and the pox carry off the young. But there must be no vanity about the daguerreotype sessions. We are not to alter our appearance with "curls" or by pinching our cheeks to make them redder or by rubbing berries over our lips to make them pink.

I wonder what Cuz Emily will see fit to adorn herself with as she sits for her daguerreotype. I was surprised to hear that she means to. A gift for Uncle Edward and Aunt Emily, she says. Well, I don't imagine she'll come as Eve! But yesterday she told me that she has become obsessed with the figure of Queen Cleopatra, often cited by Miss Lyon as an example of greatness "gone wrong." So maybe she will present herself naked in a white mantle and a crown!

I am so fatigued by her, Mamma, and all her famed "brilliance." But she may have a comeuppance tomorrow. Miss Lyon has called her in to Conference.

Your affectionate grand-daughter,
Emily Norcross

$\mathcal{D}$ear Friend Margery,

It's easier to get paper here than in most places, so I send you a line, thanking you for putting me up while I was in Northampton — and for other juicy memories I won't scarify the paper by recording. My, my, Maid Margery, we do grow sweeter every year, like a big damson plum. But how many are tasting of us, now, how many?

I've a story to tell you — you who care about educating women and women getting ahead and all that. I was in a devilish and bedeviled mood yesterday morning and started the day with a swig of rye. You know how far I've come down in the world! Once I had hopes of being a real painter, of being taken on by Mr. Joshua Johnson, the portraitist, as a pupil. I always thought of myself painting rich folks like Mr. Gilbert Stuart did or Mr. Washington Allston, and then retiring one day to Boston and a grand home. But I told you Pa was poor, we couldn't pay apprentice fees, even to the likes of Elias Richter, and so I did the next best thing and learned to work these new machines called cameras. I don't enjoy it, it's not really me that's image-making. It's all just posing the body, applying the iron headrest to fix the head, reminding the sitters not to blink or twitch, and waiting under the black cloth with your hand on the film-frame until the long long minutes are up. It's never me in it at all.

The only times I've enjoyed myself are when I can do corpses in their coffins, especially children. There's a sort of, well, *vision* required to do that well: I put white flowers, generally lilies, in the dead fingers, or I have somebody still living stand behind the corpse, for contrast. Last week, I did the portrait of a baby dead of croup and I laid her in her christening gown on her pa's knee and took him staring down at her (not crying, I stopped him from crying). I posed her clutching a teething-circle in that hard little fist of hers — stone it was, rigor having long ago set in, so I almost had to break her hand to get the teether in. But she looked like she was sleeping. Sweet Jesus, it was plaintive and sweet and heart-warming! I've gotten to be a bit famous for these Mortality Studies. They have a poetic feel.

But mostly my work is no pleasure. Carrying the equipment from town to town, putting up at hotels, bad food, boring folks. Yesterday promised to be the same or worse. If there's any subjects I despise to do, it's schoolgirls. Yesterday was Miss Mary Lyon's Seminary for Young Ladies in South Hadley, Mass., a nursery for bluestockings and missionaries. The old girl questioned me for a solid hour before she let me out the gate of her establishment — all about whether I recognized that "Man is made in God's image" and if I realized that what I would be doing was providing mere testimony to the fact. She's a real Puritan with no time for portraits, especially mechanized. And *she'd* be no subject for a camera, let me tell you, with her big wide lips, pimples and pock marks, and eyes of dull expression. An off-putter to any man, she is, and very clear to me it was, too, that to *her*, we men are the very spit of Beelzebub.

She was surrounded by a bunch of young harpies she called her assistants: so tough-looking you could get bruises just from staring at them. No, few feminine graces about Miss Lyon, I promise you. And by the way, her petticoats were dirty, which I could see when she sat herself down. On the other hand, if untidy in her dress, she is evidently a very demon of punctuality. I was late, for which she tongue-lashed me with gusto.

Anyway, I was prepared for an afternoon of sheer misery and I had it, too, about twenty young twits in pinafores, a couple of them pretty but none of them looking like they could be romanced after hours. I put that iron fixture around all their sweet necks, leaning over close to their ears, just for the kick of it, just to see if they had scent on. Not a bit of it. The headmistress keeps it so cold over yonder (you can see the Seminary from the hotel, and I found it quite mesmerizing after a time to watch the girls come out and sashay up and down the drive) that I don't think some of them had even washed in a while.

Then, just as I was so bored I could hardly speak, a thin young woman, the last on the list, slipped into the room like a swallow in a windstorm, as if she had been borne along against her will. She was paying me for my services, after all, or her father was; but she entered as if she had no rights, as if she wanted to apologize. Do you know, Marge, I felt, well, *sorry* for her. She had a graceful carriage, actually, like a dancer or one of those elocutionist girls who do little exercises to poems: the "Poetry of Motion," they call it. But she was all in brown, a wren in brown bombazine, with the crossed ribbon at the neck they all wear to seem prim. And she was white as a ghost.

"Pardon me, Sir, are you the artist?" she said.

Of course she could never have known how it plagued me to be called that, I who had failed to become one.

"Just the photographer, Miss," said I.

"But it's the same," she said brightly, in a soft, high-pitched voice. "Anyone is an artist who tries to repeat the work of Nature. So Mr. Emerson writes. Many people find it blasphemous even to try. I try every day. You are an artist if you make pictures. And I see by your equipment and mien that you do. I am only grieved to provide you with such poor raw material as myself to practice upon. I am, you know, the Only Kangaroo Among the Beauty, a kind of painful distinction. I tell myself I may be beautiful one day, but of course that is a pathetic fantasy. My other chief distinction is that I am awkward with strangers. That is why I find it so hard to talk much. Do you ever watch women talking to one another? They kiss afterward, and then go off to talk *about* each other, the traitors! Opinion is a flitting thing, but Truth outlasts the sun. Gossip is like Opinion. I would not be a Counterfeit or Plated Person. Therefore, it is so difficult for me to present myself here to be inspected. For that machine of yours will inspect me, although the real Me it cannot capture. That is within. Do *you* find it hard to talk?"

I was going to reply that no, I didn't mind talking about something important (except that hardly anything is important) when she started right up again.

"I suppose you will make me pose like all the rest? Seated in a chair with a flower in my hand and a few books at my elbow. Thus, I will seem like every other girl that's born and not like myself at all."

"How would you rather be pictured, Miss?" I said.

"Oh," she said, and dimpled, "I wish I could wear robes and a crown — for 'I have immortal longings in me'! (So Queen Cleopatra said after the death of Mark Antony. Do you love Shakespeare? I find Shakespeare the only book required. All other reading is insubstantial. Of course, this puts me at odds with many of the folk here and especially with Miss Lyon. To her, the Scriptures are Shakespeare. She prefers Moses to Orpheus, if you take my meaning. To her, the Infinite is all; but she does not perceive the Infinite in a depicted rose. It is the true artist who comprehends the Infinite. I have known all this since I was six.) But, ah, I am talking too much again. Father and Austin say I keep silent much too much; but that when I talk I talk too much. Do forgive me, Sir."

She sighed as if with the weight of all the world's troubles and then she gazed at me patiently. In all this time, I hadn't yet motioned to her to sit in the chair. Now I did. She looked at the iron headrest with its strings and bands.

"It's like some torture-apparatus Alexandre Dumas would write about. Something from the French Revolution. I suppose you tie the body down so the soul won't fly. I have observed other people's pictures. The quick runs from them right away. I shall look dead in this daguerreotype, like the image of a person without a mind. What's important is to see the visage of the Soul and not the Body's knees. I was stupid to come. But do tell me how to pose, Sir. I don't wish to be rude."

I adjusted her in the chair a hundred times without getting her to look at ease. She had an effect on me that was uncanny. I wanted so much to *comfort* her at the same time that I wanted to *throttle* her — for seeming so honest about life that I felt dishonest; for tossing all these *words* at me I couldn't understand; for being homely-handsome, virginal-voluptuous. Indeed, Margery, she really was voluptuous like some Houri behind a veil. That thin young girl, voluptuous!

She was the most recalcitrant subject I ever had to do. She objected to the fact that the books I set next to her on a table were closed. She said they should open to a page as if she had just been reading them. She said books were her "Kinsmen of the Shelf," dearer to her very often than people. She said she had picture collections of famous paintings in her house, Madonnas painted by Raphael and other papist Italians which she pored over when her father wasn't looking. Seems the Romish painters liked to show the Virgin Mary reading a book, or with a book open beside her. She said what I was doing was "right in the tradition." There was something of the schoolmarm about her. And it was as though she had been storing up things to tell me or somebody else all her life. She asked if I did photographs of the dead and when I told her yes, she burst into tears so that I had to take her out of the iron headrest, ask her what was the matter, and let her wait a bit. She said she had had a chum who had recently died. I found myself thinking "This one is passionate. This one could love a man."

But she was the very dickens to photograph. I got her back into the chair, I managed to get her to clutch some flowers. That was always my last resort, flowers, if the women were uncommon nervous. You know what she said to me? Talk about odd for a girl! She said, "Why don't you let me hold a pen in my hand, like the great George Sand?" And then she blushed beet-red.

I didn't answer to that. It was plumb peculiar, a girl wanting to be a man. I wondered if she were one of those odd man-girls you see in some cities, except that she was so gentle-looking. Anyhow, having got her settled finally, I hurried and stuck my head under the cloth and started the mechanism. Those wonderful fine, shining eyes she had (too womanly for a mere young thing like her) suddenly went dead. It was just as if I had put a knife to her heart. Her face washed out; her lips, with all the words that had danced on them, stiffened; and her eyes suddenly said nothing at all. Oh God, I was photographing a corpse without meaning to! What had I done to her?

When it was over, she said to me, very sad and forgiving-like, "Don't blame yourself if my likeness isn't lifelike. I always shrink when I feel anybody watching me. And I am rather nervous today anyway because I have a Conference with Miss Lyon tonight. I am not a favorite with her."

I wanted to ask her why, except I thought I knew. Do you see, Margery, I think this girl that I photographed may have been what is called a Genius. I haven't told you half the things she said to me — such as "The Road to Paradise is plain, but a dimpled road is more preferred." I asked her what a "dimpled road" was, and she said, "a sinful, that is to say, an exciting, that is to say a *beautiful, embellished* road. And one so tires of plainness. Do you not?" No schoolmistress could tolerate talk like that — from some girl from Amherst, which is where she hailed from. Sin as beautiful!

I don't remember when anyone drained my nerve power so much! She exhausted me, yet the odd thing is, I know I shall dream of her tonight. And I doubt I shall ever forget her calling me an "artist." Me, poor scratch of a failure, an "artist"! "We have both pledged ourselves to the spirit," she said, "we have given and taken the Ring."

Of course, she could be merely mad rather than a Genius.

But I wouldn't be surprised if that girl got ahead in the world.

Looking forward to another of our nights, Marge, with the winds outside and the sea stirring and the compass thrown away and the bed warm — wild nights, I hope.

Meanwhile, do remember

Me

*T*his evening, in only an hour's time, I must present myself before Miss Mann and Miss Lyon. They say I have much to explain. One thing is the "character of my last essay," the subject of which was Immortality.

The other! I know I shall not be able to explain the other. It is not tardiness, it is not failing to study, oh no. But it is far, far worse: the terrifying category "Communications"; for indeed I have been writing to "those outside the Seminary," and I have not given my letters to the Preceptress-Censor. Perhaps some of my letters were delivered over to her by the Postmaster of South Hadley; he is the father of one of my classmates. Indeed, I have not heard from sweet Abiah for so long! Perhaps my letters to her were confiscated! Or perhaps some of my letters to Sue . . .

I write to You, strange Love, and I am always yours. When shall we meet again, and where shall we meet, and do you know that I long for you, ever and ever? In my dreams I always come to you

> In white,
> *Emily*

*M*y wheel is in the dark!
I cannot see a spoke

My heart is in the dark.
I see better there.

My eye is in the dark,
A Samson misery

My foot is on the Tide!

Danger is the sweet Heart
Of Pleasure, and thrilling Sister
To Joy.

Conformity is
Misery
Art is
Unconformity . . .
Art is
Ecstasy . . .

*M*y dear Eustacia,

There have been times over the years when I have been shaken in my convictions.

Today I feel very shaken indeed; for certain events taking place here have put me in mind of you. Indeed, so heavy is my heart this day that I write to you, Eustacia, thus presuming on our old affection. One cannot always be silent. One cannot always be prudent.

Did you know that for many years it was painful to me to hear your name spoken, or to read of you in the gazette, or to be told anything at all about Nantucket Seminary for Young Ladies, or of your achievements in founding it or running it, without a lump in my throat? You remember still, you must! how we had planned to establish a school for young ladies *together* and that it had been the dearest wish of our hearts. But then you left suddenly, you left me, Eustacia, and really it nearly destroyed me. I am still sick to death when I remember it. Sometimes I imagine that no success in my endeavors will ever make up to me for the loss of you; for the loss of our love for each other! (*There!* I have said it.) Prayer has not sufficed to erase your image from my heart. Though I chide my too-faithful affection with recollections of the sarcasm and condescension and, yes, *cruelty,* that you showed me in those last days, I cannot forget the dawn of love. Your early sweetness, like a flower! And I mourn you still.

Well, doubtless I shall bore you if I go on; you always thought me too earnest, I well recall. Nor do I mean to fill these pages with recriminations. I have been reminded of you, I have been reminded of *us*, by something that happened here yesterday, by an interview I had with one of the students. I will not tell you her name, lest it should come out when and if you should meet someone in her family. They are well connected. She is seventeen, in the Junior class, and bright. Had she not been placed with the rather humorless literature mistress who makes most of the complaints I receive about her, the girl might not have run into so much trouble. She's by no means a *bad* girl, but she has independent notions, will take very little on faith, is dutiful but inquisitive. And she reads constantly. Not only the books we assign, but many others, all of them too adult for such a youthful person, and many that are undignified or even unsavory in content. (We think her brother brings them to her.) Miss Mann, the English mistress, has been convinced from the first that the girl cheats in writing essays and cribs what she writes from what she reads. She imagines this because the girl's essays are so developed, so imaginative, and sometimes so completely without modesty. She will describe the emotions that lead to marriage, for example, as if she knows what they are. (*Does* she?) In addition, to the central program of the Seminary, the formation of Christian souls, she is largely indifferent. She will never be a believer, I think, though she composes airy verses on the loveliness of Nature in which some sort of divine principle patterned on Mr. Emerson's vaporous Deity seems to be in evidence.

We had a meeting with her, Miss Mann and I, to discover whether she was a cheater. She had written an essay on Immortal Life that was so clever, we could only believe she had gotten it from some philosopher whose texts were unfamiliar to us. She had submitted the essay just after a remarkable act of insubordination, the theft of sweets on quite a large scale. (The more I ponder the latter, I think she may have stolen them to win the other girls' love. She is a very needy person for all her cleverness. Evidently, she meant to share what she stole.) But we are wrong to imagine that she cheats, I am sure! For to every question we put to her, she returned an utterly brilliant answer, uniquely couched in extraordinary words. I have never heard anything like such language from any girl before. Of course, I am not glad of that! Such wit may not equip her to be happy in this life. Wit is not for women. What we must have is the strength to suffer, is it not so? One of her replies, moreover, was truly impious. When I asked her straight out how she came by such original notions, she said she was "inspired." Of course I snapped right back severely that saints and geniuses might be inspired but not little seventeen-year-old girls from Amherst.

But now I come to what so moved me to write to you.

She has been sending letters to young girls round about. Of course such correspondence is quite forbidden. Many of her letters to one young lady — more than fifteen! — were put into my hands by the Postmaster here. They are letters that will make her entirely . . . misunderstood. They are the sort of letters you and I wrote to each other long ago at school. Oh, do you remember? And she writes them openly. Indeed, she wrote, knowing that letters may be opened here and that she could be severely punished for writing without my permission.

Eustacia, they are beautiful letters. Ardor unabashed, though not yet quite self-aware. You will not, I daresay, recall Lago di Como or the *billets-doux* you often left under my pillow during our sojourn in that earthly Paradise. Her letters were like yours. Perhaps you and Miss Harriet Gibbon, your co-foundress, go to the old villa there together now, with no thought of your abandoned Mary!

I scolded the girl savagely for writing those letters. I mocked her for addressing words of love to someone of her own sex. I reminded her that she was seventeen and that girlish enthusiasms were meant to give way by that age to the serious reflection and mature ardor that result in marriage. In short, I behaved like a hypocrite and a liar.

But what should I have done, Eustacia? She is, I fear, what some call "an artist." The passions run high in such breasts. She is deeply in when it comes to this girl to whom she writes. By the way, I have forbidden that, now, on pain of expulsion. She turned quite pale to be told there could be no more letters. Then I longed to take her in my arms and tell her that I understood what she was experiencing but that God had forbidden such emotions! Ah, Eustacia, how hard life is!

Well, none of this will interest you, I suppose.

Miss Mann, by the way, envious (I think) of the girl's imagination, has told her we would continue to watch for signs of dishonesty in her essays. And she pressed me to press the girl to come to some final decision about joining the church, which the girl has refused so far to do. How all this will end, I do not know.

Her father is one of our chief donors, a very powerful man.

I am afraid to break her spirit entirely.

Remember me sometimes, Eustacia, and that I think of you.

Mary

I have come back from The Inquiry. I am as unhappy as They could mean me to be.

To You, from Whom I keep nothing and will never
keep what touches me, to You I must talk, now, or my
heart will surely break!

How did you help Geoffrey and William and John?
How did you comfort all those souls on fire for very love
of you? I am in love and need comfort.

They brought me into the room and the room was
very spare. (They always do that. Miss Mann observes
that Miss Lyon likes to adorn her chambers with flowers before any spiritual interrogation, as if she were
readying the soul for Christ the bridegroom. But I have
never noticed much decoration. The rooms are swept
bare and they are cold.) I have noted for a long while
that my room in Father's house is motionless as stone
and the view outside my window remains ever the
same: the tree at the very same angle, with the light
crazing the birch as if it were enamel, and beyond it,
the church spire. Yet my room at home is crammed
with enchantments. There are my hyacinths on the
night-table in winter, and in the summer the geraniums
crowding the sill. There are the birds outside, soaring
into the heavens, each one with a thought of me.

They asked me how I had managed to write so
"stirringly" about eternal life. I said that it was not
difficult since I feel I am always tending toward that

shore in my dreams. They asked whether it was not Miss Lyon's teachings that had prompted my thoughts, and I replied honestly, "No." They asked next if Miss Lyon's teachings were anything to me at all. And I said, "All you teach us about the beauty of gathering flowers, dear Miss Lyon, I have taken much to heart." Then they asked, "Who wrote your essay on Eternity, Emily? We cannot believe you capable of those grand sentences yourself."

And so I told them, very truly, that You wrote my essay.

After that all went very cruelly for me and they asked about Sue.

We have spoken of her, You and I. You know I am not stupid. I see her in the years ahead. I see what she will be to me. A little while from now she will give up her coldness toward me; she will be fond of me. And then, I shall become even more dazzled by her. Because I am dazzled, she will turn on me; she will give me up. I see the picture of What Will Be. I will be sitting in my square and stone-like room with its fragrance of enchantment and Sue will be waiting on a step outside a door not far from mine. She will wait for a carriage full of furs and jewels and children to take her to a ball where someone else will kiss her on the lips. I will feel that kiss, though I may never give it.

Yet Sue will grant me something, I do not yet know what. And I shall continue to write to her, despite all that Miss Lyon demands. Indeed, I must *see* her.

Now what do you think of my thoughts, you who seem to know the future?

*W*e have just finished dinner here, Austin, and I longed to write to you so much all through Miss Lyon's accompanying talk on Caring for the Poor that I hurried back to my room where I seat myself to address you.

It is painful to me to think how long it may be before I am allowed to come home. The examinations commence here — the examinations for entrance to the Senior form — on February seventh, after which I might be permitted a holiday. Oh, Austin, I am very miserable! You well remember, I am sure, how you yourself experienced such pangs when you were away at school.

I have nothing cheerful to report about our life here.

Did you see Sue Gilbert, as you planned, last week? Hers is a rare and special nature, and a character that Father would approve, I think. Do you know that she writes poetry, as you and I do? Have you written any verses lately, Austin? If you do, will you send them here? Father lives for one of your poems and thinks you greatly gifted. He says your poems and even your letters are altogether better than Shakespeare. He wants to have them published and kept in our library. Now, Brother Pegasus, I've been in the habit myself of writing a few things, and it rather appears to me that you're stealing away my patent, so you'd better be somewhat careful, or I'll call the police! Ah, how I do become the Shadow Lady that lives in your shadow!

But I miss your hurrahs, dear Austin, and the famous stir you always make!

You say in your last that you would have me be more "ordinary" in my conduct and language as befits a young lady of excellent manners. You tell me to be "simple," as befits a woman. There are others — some of them very near at hand — who counsel me in the same fashion. *You* seem to want me to be a little ninny, a little pussy catty, a little Red Riding Hood, with a Bee in my Bonnet and a Rosebud in my hair. You want me to be "ordinary," you say? Was Queen Elizabeth the First ordinary? Was Joan of Arc? Was Cleopatra?

I strive and struggle and climb to reach the clouds while you stroll out in your slippers from your masculine perch upon Empyrean and tell me to get down . . . and be "simple"!

Yet I do miss you, Austin. I wish I might tell you some of what has happened to me here. I think you would pity me. By the way, there has been a Menagerie here this week. Miss Lyon, to our great surprise, permitted the girls to go out and see the bears, monkeys, etc, if they desired. Almost all the girls went. But I stayed behind and enjoyed the Solitude finely! I care not for Bears, but for the Birds of the Spirit!

Please, Austin, will you ask Susie to come and see me? I believe you like Susie. It would not be hard for you to stop by at William Cutler's one day and leave her a note. There is a coach that comes by the Sem each Sunday from Amherst. I believe Father and Mother know of it. Do implore Sue to come and visit me, her homesick friend.

Affy yr sister,
Emilie

*D*ear Friend Emily,

I have waited some months to reply to your last.

I did find comical your account of your bad cold, which made your cousin Emily climb into the currant bushes outside your window to get away from your sneezes. You said that that was a "wicked story," but I did not find it so, dear Emily. What did, and *does,* trouble me, though, is all that followed, about snakes, and stories, and Christ Our Lord! I do not comprehend what you say about your stories being flowers of speech that make and also tell "deliberate falsehoods" but that you love them anyhow, though you would have *me* avoid all such falsehood! What did you mean? "The big serpent bites the deepest," you say, "and we get so accustomed to its bites that we don't mind about them." Who and what is the big serpent? Emily, you do not mean the devil, do you? What do you know about *him?* I do not think you should write of "Christ's temptations, and how they were like our own" and wonder if any of them made him "angry"! Christ was perfect, Emily, he was never angry! How can you go on so?

You write of our old friend Abby "full of radiance" as "a sweet girl Christian." You did make her sound so strange, Emily. It frightens me to hear you call yourself "one of the lingering bad ones." Emily, you must take some account of your inner life. What is to become of you? No one from school will want to speak to you if you go on like this about snakes, and blaspheming the Lord. Unless, of course, you mean to confine your attentions to that sharp-tongued Sue Gilbert. I guess with her background — her pa, a drunk (there, I should not have written that but it's true!), and her guardian, a miserly, ill-tempered old crittur — I guess she would understand the wild language you customarily employ. I can't abide it!

You ask me where I am and where my thoughts are and you demand where are my "young affections" and say you hope they are "not with the *boots* and *whiskers.*" Well, there are a pair of boots and there is one set of whiskers to which I am, I think, becoming devoted. But there, I cannot tell *you*, Emily, any of this, for I do believe you are unsympathetic to love! You do not seem to love anyone, yet, of the Stronger Sex I find so admirable. Shall that day ever come for you, I wonder! Shall you never be a bride in white? Shall you never know the peace and gladness of a good man's affection? Sometimes I fall asleep at night and dream of my Samuel's face; it is strong, like his name, and so beautiful! He has not asked me, yet. But I hope that he will. There. I have written of him, though I said I would not! Pray do not be offended. I know you do not like to hear about beaux.

You say you wish we could all remain mere children and you ask if I do not feel the same. Oh no, dear Emily, I do not. I yearn to have children of my own. One cannot *be* a child and have a child!

I do not know if I will visit you in Amherst as you

asked this summer. Events may occur that will prevent me. It is also hard for me to write quite so often as you demand, for I have many duties after school.

I pray for you, Emily.

Abiah Palmer Root

Postscript: It is not kind, but I must add that Sue Gilbert seems to me vain and avaricious. It may be your father's hospitality she is after, not your friendship. And you have an unwed brother, Emily, your father's heir. Perhaps she means to marry him and improve her condition. How sad that you prefer her now to all your old friends!

I think I do not sufficiently seduce you.

How may I do so? Am I not a wise young lady in some ways? Am I not a Queen for you to play King to? Am I not more a Queen, even, than Sue? Say it! But my studies are nothing to me if I think of you. Once, at the blackboard, when the Geometry mistress was guiding my hand, the sable before me lightened, and I saw your Face.

I live with You, I see your Face, I sleep but then I wake in my sleep. And in my Dream,

> Do Thee distinguished Grace —
> Till jealous Daylight interrupt —
> And mar thy perfectness —

That is a poem. I try to make them now.

I mean to alter my rhetoric so that Persons of Note will take note of me. (I do not mean my teachers.) Then you will embrace me more often! I do not believe you could love women who write to you in the way Miss Mann prefers. She is a poor deaf creature without ears to hear; the Word does not sing for her. I try to obey her, though she mocks me every day. To my astonishment, she offered me a poem yesterday that she herself wrote and asked me what I thought of it. "You are a very good woman," I said, "Miss

Mann, but one must tell the truth. These verses do not breathe." Her face contracted with rage and now I am in disgrace.

> Thine, in white,
> *Emily*

$\mathcal{D}$ear Mr. Higginson,

Thank you for yours of the twenty-fifth December. I still do not celebrate a "feast" on the day in question, being loyal to the principles of Mary Lyon.

If your experience of Miss Emily Dickinson differs from my own, it may be because she was successful in lying to you, cheating you. Us, she could *not* cheat. She was sometimes dutiful, I do not deny it. And we never proved, precisely, that she was copying her essays from anyone else's. But I had many opportunities in the spring of 1848 to see with what levity she regarded all Virtue! "The little tippler leaning against the sun," her poem says. Well, I don't think she was a drinker. She was other things. You once told me about Judge Otis Lord's regard for her; that he wanted to marry her when he was in his dotage and she was forty-eight or so. But I wonder if you have heard what the niece of Judge Otis Lord said about her? She called her "a little hussy, crazy about men." I heard that from a neighbor woman, here, who knew the niece. The niece was Miss Abby Farley. You being so well connected, you would know about the Judge better than I, and how famous he was. But he was also a friend of old Mr. Dickinson, and after his wife died, he may have been looking for a housekeeper. Anyway, it certainly angered Miss Abby to know that her uncle was wooing a cracked old spinster who hadn't come out of her house into the daylight for fifteen years!

Now, how do you suppose Emily got old Judge Lord to propose marriage to her? How do you suppose that, despite that plain pinched face of hers, she could have interested him?

Even the best of people have been known to conceal lurid desires.

In my opinion, Emily Dickinson was a witch. I think she put Judge Lord under a spell. I think he looked to her for fascinations he had dreamt of and never known in his honest life. For she was *not honest* and this was clear to us even when she was a child.

I give you just one example. I was friendly that spring of '48 with the Mathematics mistress. Miss Lyon firmly believed that young ladies should proceed in the Mathematics as far as the Calculus, exactly like their brothers. Some educators said her idea was ridiculous. Why prepare women so arduously for doing household accounts? But Miss Lyon was a true bluestocking.

Anyway, Miss Pettibone and I were friendly. It was a friendship of opposites, certainly, since Miss Pettibone was not creative like me, she had none of my fondness for poetry. But she was a woman of the highest principle. Emily Dickinson had been in Miss Pettibone's algebra class, a quite indifferent student. In the Spring term she proceeded to geometry. In some ways at first, she seemed better able in that class, perhaps because there one was allowed to use words. But Clara Pettibone came to me one day in January with a dreadful story. There had been a test. Each girl was sent to the blackboard to solve a problem involving the isosceles triangle. Emily Dickinson was assigned a most ordinary problem. But after saying "superimpose two triangles," which was the first line of the proposition to be memorized the week before, she fell silent. (Clara said Emily loved the word "superimpose" and indeed all of the terms of the Mathematics — "logarithm" was a favorite — and would hang on to them like a drowner; but she never appeared interested in working out the problems numerically.) Clara Pettibone demanded, "Please continue, Miss Dickinson, you are supposed to have prepared this theorem," and Emily Dickinson said then, "I know, Miss Pettibone, but I find myself more interested in the circle than the triangle. The circle is the symbol of Infinity. In my opinion, we should spend more of our time at the Seminary considering the properties of the circle, since Miss Lyon is so eager to prepare us for eternal life."

No one had asked her for her opinion.

The other girls laughed; they were shocked by her pertness. Clara Pettibone did not laugh.

"The solution to the proposition, please, Emily, right now!" she said to her. There was a pause and then Emily Dickinson gabbled a solution so fast that Clara wasn't certain she had even heard it. She made Emily repeat it. It was a very unconventional solution, but you could not — technically — say it wasn't right. What it was was a *strange* solution. Yet the fact is there was no way she could have learned it from Clara or from the textbook. Somebody must have given it to her. She must have been getting outside help. She wasn't able to do the proposition as they did it in the book, either! So you see, she was cheating. She must have been.

Her cousin Emily Norcross, whom I liked, as I told you earlier, said to Miss Pettibone, "Cousin Emily Dickinson is never floored by anything. She doesn't believe in being floored."

Every decent human being is "floored" by something.

She did that problem by cheating or she did it by magic.

If you imagine she is so good, Mr. Higginson, then how is it she never took any of your kind advice about her writing? "The Nun of Amherst," you say she's called. I know little of the Roman Catholics. I am a good Quaker woman. But nuns are, I hear, women who take direction from their superiors. Everyone knows who reads the papers that Emily Dickinson wrote to you for counsel about her writing and then never took the advice you gave! I see in *The Northampton Gazette* that you told her to correct her grammar, to write regular rhymes, to give up her strange ways of putting things — ways she had, even as a child. But she flouted you altogether, I understand, and even used to send you versions of your own poems, done up as *she* preferred, not as you did! Impious, disrespectful little baggage!

In February of that spring term of 1848, we discovered her writing what were even then called "Valentines" — not only to some mysterious person whom she would not call by name, but to a *girl* in Amherst, the same we ultimately caught her with behind a closed door a few days later. What she was doing behind that closed door, I would be sick to tell you. Sending Valentines, not to speak of writing them, was strictly forbidden. But for her to have encouraged a secret visit, and one that took the form that visit took! Her wickedness was a great shock to Miss Lyon. And for Emily, it hastened the end, as far as we were concerned. I was not sorry.

Well, I am elderly and frail, now, and it is hard for me to write these letters.

Do you know what my own life has been? I, too, had ambition once. I would have liked to be a writer and I might have been a good and successful one who earned money and applause. But I never had the chance. I always had to teach and earn my living. While that girl Dickinson lived in luxury in Squire Dickinson's big house, and could write whatever she wanted all day long, I was drumming their lessons into the dolts at the Seminary. Years and years of teaching dolts and eating porridge and mouthing hymns. Do you know what it does to you? It withers you up; it turns you to vinegar!

Now I live here in Northampton, a few miles from Emily Dickinson's grave. I read about her funeral in the newspaper six years ago, and I saw all the compliments her sister-in-law paid her in her obituary! More lies! Everybody knew they *hated* each other at the end! After all, they had been each other's tempters! Did you know that they hated each other?

Last Saturday, I had an impulse. I left this house in which I live — half-house, actually, I have the little upper story under the attic — and I took the Coach to Emily Dickinson's fine grave, where she is buried in luxury next to her parents, real luxury with a decorated iron fence around the plots. And I seized a clump of dirt and I hurled it on to her headstone. At last I had lifted my hand against her, and was content.

Only charity keeps me from continuing. It is strange, but the more I correspond with you, Mr. Higginson, the more convinced I am that I was right about Emily Dickinson; and the more I read your excuses for her, the more deluded I think you are! I may have been tortured in my soul when I began this correspondence. But now, thrashing it all out with you, I see clearly that I was right. Indeed, I am beginning to gloat — yes, *gloat* — about my own good judgment!

Sincerely,
Margaret Mann

*M*y dear Austin,

Your *welcome* letter found me all engrossed in the history of Sulphuric Acid!!!! I deliberated a few moments after its reception on the propriety of carrying it to one of the teachers; we are supposed to give our mail up to the Censor. But the result of my deliberation was a conclusion to open it with moderation, peruse its contents with sobriety becoming my station, & if after a close investigation I found nothing which savored of rebellion or an unsubdued will, to lay it away in my folio & forget I had ever received it.

Are you not gratified that I am so rapidly gaining correct ideas of female propriety & sedate deportment? That is, that I am learning to efface myself at all times and subdue my wicked human desires? Women, they say, should have limited contact with WORDS; for words are lively as serpents and apt to kill. I am Eve reincarnate, as I told you once, however. Serpents do not scare me. If a word has not the power to kill, it should never be uttered.

I am ever more lonely; but cheered by the thought that Father does not intend me to return here for a second year, I take comfort & I hope on. How did you manage to persuade him to let me come home for good? Or was it Mother, fearing for my health? Miss Lyon will never understand, for the chief purpose —

she thinks — for my being here has not been fulfilled: I have not yet declared for Christ!

I suppose you have written many Valentines. Here in South Hadley, Valentine's takes a whole week. But every night I have looked in vain for one of Cupid's messengers. Many of the girls have received very beautiful ones & I have not done hoping for one. I entreat you to tell your friend Thomas, who used to like me (I thought), that I am pining for a Valentine. Probably Abby and Sister Viny have received scores of Valentines from the infatuated wights in the neighborhood while your *highly accomplished & gifted elder sister* is entirely overlooked. How I do long to be the object of desire to someone! How splendid it would be to know oneself adored! Oh, I do think Love the most engaging of the heavenly virtues. Yes, "the greatest of these is Charity." Now *that is a gospel message to which I could adhere.* For if one were loved, she could never be lonely.

Monday afternoon Mistress Lyon arose in the hall & forbade our sending "any of those foolish notes called Valentines." But the girls who were here last year, knowing her opinions, were sufficiently cunning to write & give them into the care of Dickinson during the vacation, so that I despatched about 150 on Valentine morn, before orders could be put down to the contrary! Hearing of this act, Miss Whitman, Mistress Lyon's assistant, with frowning brow, sallied over to the Post Office to ascertain if possible the number of Valentines and — worse still — the name of the offending Postmistress: me! Nothing has yet been heard as to what she learned. Dickinson was a good hand to help the girls, don't you agree?

Strange, I try to be a good friend to all here, but they do not seem to care for me very much. I do not seem made in their mold, Austin. I would I were a blonde and plump, as is the fashion; or I would my hair were raven black like Sue's. I should really like to be The Belle of Amherst.

I have had a severe cold for a few days. It is freezing weather here, which — together with the fact that I have received no message of love from any soul at all — makes me *hungrier than usual, and as you well know, I am ever famished.*

Do not show this letter to anyone, Austin, and do not scold me for my Valentine prank. Do not show it to Sue. I want her to think me popular.

Do you see her very often? Madeleine Carbury said she saw you two walking together on the Common. Sue was wearing her feathered hat, in which she seems (to me) like some medieval princess. You had your heads together and she was listening to your low-spoken words. Your brow was contracted in a black frown, and once you put your arm around her waist. Ah, how bold you are, Austin, like a knight in a poem!

Does Sue miss her Emily?

Your affectionate sister

No Passenger was known to flee
Who sailed with her in Ecstasy,
No Captain could escape a shore
Where her Heart lodged evermore.

Yet he, the Darker Spirit bold,
Rude and false to the Captain mild,
Fingered her Breast to mar its grace,
Bloodied her life to own her Face.

$\mathcal{D}$ear Emily,

Your Valentine arrived while I was stooped over the laundry tubs. I did not at first recognize the hand and hoped, actually, it was sent by Austin! We have been seeing a good deal of each other lately. Then, when I unsealed the letter and read the salutation, I knew such extravagance could only come from you.

Dear Emily, it has always been most kind of you to take such an interest in me and I do reciprocate your warm friendship. We all need friends. I always admire your writing style. Sometimes it seems like a thunder-bolt, sometimes like a rose rimmed by rainbow clouds, sometimes like a parson fashioning epigrams. You are right to think that I am impressed. Sometimes after I read one of your letters or verses I sit down and try to write like you myself. So catching is your style that I am often successful. I doubt even you yourself could tell the difference between your poems and some of my copies of them. Thus I do find your affection valuable.

But I must ask that you not embarrass me with ex-cess of devotion. Your letters . . . they are more *hot* than they should be, even between devout friends. Please be more cautious. William often reads my mail. What might he think? You know those two schoolteachers in Northampton who were disgraced. Do you want to seem like *them?* Do not call me "Queen." Should you not bend your efforts to finding some swain who might give you that title himself?

You say you long for a Valentine and yet you say you fear being "yielded up to the man of Noon." My, my, how poetical you are. You see yourself as a flower fainting in the heat of masculine desire, do you? For me, I am not afraid of men, nor have I any special fondness for them. Any man who hurts me will get back worse than he gave. I am no fainting flower. My father was a disappointment to us, our brothers forget me I often think, and my brother-in-law Cutler is a martinet. I may be "only seventeen," as you say, but women were married, were mothers, and were buried by that age a hundred years ago. I am as old as you seem young. I am terribly old. It comes of privation.

As for women, they draw me scarcely at all. They are so often silly. Do you know what I care for? Things. Books. Objects. Porcelain, for example. Fabrics. Horses. Gems. The sunset. If I could *own something!* To lay my hand on property: this would seem better to me than any human love.

I gather from some of the verses you send me that you do not feel the same, except about the sunset. You sound very ascetic.

You must forget about exchanging kisses last summer. It was mere whimsy, mere caprice on my part, and meant nothing. I do not know even how it came about. It was only my wish to be kind to you when you turned your face into mine.

What a strong, headstrong, but sensitive young man is your brother, Austin! I think he may be very successful at the Law. He says, Emily, that you wish me to pay you a visit at the Seminary on my way to New York in a few days. I shall consider it and send a message to you by Hepzibah Gates, who is going to Hadley to nurse her sister. I should like to please Austin's sister, if nothing else! I am not without warmth of heart. I hope Miss Lyon don't intercept this letter.

Sue

*S*he has answered me and this time, kindly!

God gives us many cups. From what wassail will you drink with me? This world is short. There is not time enough for all I must do, and ever at my back I hear the famous chariot.

If she comes to see me, my life will be set on its course.

Do you mean her to come? If she comes, you must not forsake me.

For you are ever Alpha and Omega.

Emily

$\mathcal{D}$ear Mamma,

Emily Dickinson may be my cousin, but I don't wish to know her after we part at the term's end. She is not returning to Miss Lyon's next year, did you hear? Of course, since I shall be graduating in May, I should not have been in her company anyhow. But in the last few weeks she has so disgraced herself that I do not wish to maintain a friendship even outside these walls. Do not object to this, Mamma, for she is a wild girl and I will not be painted with her brush!

Now, Mamma, does Uncle Edward know all she is guilty of? Is that why she is not returning here? Or are the Dickinsons pretending to take her home for her health? Everyone whispers and gossips about her.

The worst of it started around Valentine's when she did her prank of mailing scores of lovelorn messages from the other girls to boys in our neighborhood. This was strictly forbidden. We may not have tender correspondence with men. But Emily is not popular, her ideas are too original. She did this, I know, to win some affection. Well, her design failed because we were all punished with the guilty ones after Miss Whitman learned their names; and then the girls blamed Emily for volunteering her services. (Do you know she calls herself "Dickinson" now, as if she were a boy? Yesterday she told me she wished she were married to Elizabeth Barrett Browning, who she thinks is a marvelous poet. She is so odd! Miss Lyon wonders, I think, how Emily gets hold of all these new poets' books — she must have them smuggled in by Austin because she has read the very latest poetry. Worse still, she has read the most fashionable novels, she reads them at night when she thinks I am asleep, and then — since she has wasted so much candle light — our room is put on short rations of dessert to make up the expense of new candles.)

Still, she is not in disgrace for either of these bad acts. There is something else she has done, something so terrible that nobody knows what it is. She is allowed to go to classes, but if you could see, Mamma, how Miss Mann regards her when she enters the Literature room, you would be astounded. Why, it is as if Miss Mann had seen a bug with large crawling jelly eyes walking along the wall! I would die of mortification if Miss Mann looked like that at me. But Emily just bears up bravely, though her lip trembles and she does get thinner, it seems, with every passing day. Her English compositions are just as "rare," I mean weird, as ever. It is such a disgrace to be related to her if you are studying English!

But I think there is a look of . . . well, exultation about Emily lately, as if she has been singled out! Singled out for what, I should like to know!

And now, tonight, Mamma, Miss Lyon holds a last meeting with those who have not yet declared for Christ. Emily Dickinson must attend, she cannot be excused. Of course she will never relent and behave like an honorable young woman and a Christian! Instead, she will not rise to take the oath, she will refuse to be saved, and thus she will further disgrace our whole family. Indeed, Mamma, could you not have made sure of her character before you insisted that I live and sleep with Emily Dickinson for one whole year?

Your distressed grand-daughter,
Emily

My dear Miss Mann,

Your letter of the fifth January seemed to summon me into a different age and — forgive me — a harsher world. Though the genius of the Puritans, manifested so chastely in the works of Emerson, has given much to the American spirit, the atmosphere you describe at Mary Lyon's Seminary speaks to me not of Emerson but of a darker, more morbid Puritan influence: Hawthorne's.

My friend Emily Dickinson was, she once told me, "enticed" by Hawthorne; yet she also found his obsession with crime and with sin "appalling." Hers was a gentle, optimistic, child-like personality in many respects. I cannot say how wrong I think you are in your suppositions about her nature. A "witch"! Surely, Miss Mann, you were ill when you wrote that phrase. I doubt that Emily Dickinson possessed much sense of evil at all. She was too sheltered, too good a person, to know about evil, except insofar as it appeared in the form of weeds in her garden. Well, certainly she knew about evil from her reading. Did you know that she admired mystery and crime stories, as so many of us do? I always found it droll that she was so well acquainted with the latest murder in Amherst, she whose brow was as unclouded by untoward desire as a summer sky!

But in strict confidentiality I will tell you, too, that there was one form of evil that she seems to have known intimately and completely despised; and that was falsehood. About falsehood, one member of her family — her sister-in-law — taught her all too much. (I have this from a most reliable and disinterested source, Mrs. Mabel Loomis Todd. Mrs. Todd, my fellow editor of the *Poems*, was at first a friend of Mrs. Austin Dickinson. She still cares for her. But she has withdrawn from their friendship because of Mrs. Dickinson's fondness for untruths. Mrs. Todd was informed by Miss Lavinia Dickinson, her sister's life-long companion, that the calumnies Mrs. Austin spread about Mrs. Todd were matched in their vindictiveness by the lies she uttered about Miss Emily. And Miss Emily deplored *all* Mrs. Austin's lies.) You may imagine, therefore, how astonished I am that you would accuse the young Emily Dickinson of cheating! She always had an heroic regard for Truth, it is one of her major themes in the poetry.

In fact, if she did not (as you report) join the church under Miss Lyon's influence, I attribute it to her personal integrity. She would not say she believed what she did not believe, even to make her life easier. And if she was able to do a difficult geometry theorem well, I ascribe it to her natural brilliance. She was remarkably ingenious, a strong thinker if a poor rhymer. In fact, some of her poems seem to me like geometrical theorems: "If your Soul seesaw, / Lift the Flesh door," goes one; and another is about "soldered mouths," and a number of them are definitions that read like equations, often worked out with a sort of mathematical and cryptic condensation. I don't think she ever copied anything. "I like the look of agony," she writes, "Because I know it's true." Truth was everything to her. I think she never took my advice, as you rightly point out, because it would have constituted a lie for her to act as though what worked for me worked for her.

I wished I might have been more to her; done more for her!

Finally, Miss Mann, Emily Dickinson was her own person. She wrote for herself. It seems that you found that impious in her, even when she was a girl. But I must remind you that Genius always seeks its own path. To me, she was a kind of genius. Time will tell if I am right.

Her father, you may not know, once had a local minister interrogate Emily Dickinson about Christian dogma. This minister is said to have found her "sound" in every respect. I do recall that she would not go to church after her thirtieth year; but she rarely went any-where after 1860. Not even across the lawn to her sister-in-law's. (Of course, there may be an *histoire* when it comes to that. I expect this is what you mean when you say that Mrs. William Austin Dickinson — Sue — and Emily Dickinson "hated" one another. My dear friend was not malicious enough to hate anyone. But certainly she had come to fear Mrs. Austin before her life ended. How sad that was, I have not eloquence enough to relate!)

I have never been a teacher, Miss Mann, unless one regards writing essays as teaching, and thus I cannot imagine how a pupil might remain in the mind to dis-tress me, even after the pupil is several years dead! It is clear to me that your feelings about Emily Dickinson arise in part from personal unhappiness. May I make one remark that may be helpful to you? In your first letter you observed that I am a minister. Allow me to minister to you for a moment.

You appear to resent what you consider Emily Dickinson's wealth. You imagine her life to have been one of no labor. But that is not true. Although Squire Dickinson was not wealthy, he was well-off. However, he took the position of many men in the '60s, that his daughters had to work alongside their servants. There were eight Irish servants, but Emily Dickinson did all the baking in her father's house. I remember telling you that once already. From her fifteenth year, she canned fruit and she also picked the fruit from the trees with her father's day laborers. I have many a letter from her about being freckled from the effort — as you know, she was exceptionally fair-skinned. When her mother had a stroke in the '70s, it was Emily who became her nurse. Mrs. Dickinson was partially paralyzed and — though Miss Dickinson never complained of it — very hard to lift, to feed, to please. I do not know how she managed, even, to write poetry, so many and harsh were her duties.

How different, in short, was the woman I knew and admired from the girl you disparage. I can only hope to receive no more letters from you like your last.

Sincerely,
Thomas Wentworth Higginson

Postscript: Miss Lavinia told me once that, accused of being "queer" for not joining the church, Emily Dickinson had said simply, "I thought a lie would be queerer." This is what I mean about her truthfulness. I just recall it.

$\mathcal{D}$ear Sue,

I am at my window, leaning so far out that I can smell the raindrops that linger in the trees. We have had a storm, but now the crimson children are playing in the West. What I am gazing at would please you: a sunset so rich, so radiant, that it could be your own raiment, my Queen, my Friend! At moments like these, I feel no need of other Heaven than this one below!

You say you will be here in a few days. On Sunday. Oh happy Sun-Day!

Now, Susie, it is wrong to lie, to be disobedient, to be stealthy, and yet we must. Truth is important; but Love is more than Truth. So you must dress in your darkest garments and wait until it is night to approach the Seminary. You know we are allowed no visitors, save on holidays, no one at all except our parents. My window is the third from the left on the ground floor back. There is a garden door adjoining, the key to which I have stolen from Miss Whitman's chain, left at her place at dinner and claimed instantaneously by Dickinson! I shall open the garden door for you and be waiting. Cousin Emily will not be here, she is gone to Monson for a tooth extraction. We will have the night to talk in and, like Romeo, you can leave before the dawn and fetch up for breakfast at the hotel. Of course, you are really Juliet to my Romeo. Or we are both Romeo and Juliet together, I think. (I know you will not like my saying this; you will find it "extravagant." But I see us as the only poets, and so *they* were to one another. You constitute poetry for me! Do not fear that I love you over-much, Sue. I realize that you must marry some day and leave me quite forlorn. But we must live in the Here and Now!)

Oh, Susie, do not fail to come and succor
Emily

*M*y dear Eustacia,

Of course I have had no reply from you to my last letter, though that did not surprise me. I hope you take note that I send all my letters to you under another's superscription: Miss Whitman is kind enough to inscribe your name on the envelopes without asking me why such subterfuge is required. This letter will be hand-delivered by my old nurse, whom I trust completely. Therefore, I will allow myself to speak to you one last time, even as one might speak after a desperate silence.

I remember that you once told me — terrible memory! — how Harriet burned every token of me or mine that you possessed when she came to live with you. That you were "afraid" to write to me! And that she never gave you those few letters I sent in the beginning, when my heart was full to breaking, after we parted! Perhaps you will be angry that I am writing to you once more. I well recall how easily I could anger you. (So much about me angered you at last: my intelligence, my eagerness to succeed, qualities that drew you to me in the beginning and that you held cheap at the end.) But I cannot refrain from writing; for you were my whole Life once, and certain events of late remind me too compellingly of the fact. Harriet has nothing to fear from me now, and I know all too well that I have become Nothing to *you!* Yet I yearn to confide, Eustacia, these events that recall me to what we once felt for one another. I see ourselves so clearly as we were. Ah, it is a pitiable irony, a tangled web!

The young girl I wrote to you of in January has enticed and received a forbidden visitor here. You know my rules: they are almost the same ones that Miss Vulpet made for us when we were girls at Harrison Sem. "No special friends, no private letters, no beaux." And how we laughed, do you remember, to think that her rules — devised to frustrate the seductive trickery of the Stronger Sex — were useless when it came to the True Affection women like ourselves experience for one another? Men were forbidden; but it was not forbidden to *us* to do such tender acts as lovers do! I could clasp your hand each morning when we awoke with no fear of reprisal, kiss you endlessly without fear of condemnation! Forgive me for remembering, but there are days when I can almost *feel* your hand in my hair, Eustacia, days when at the least convenient moment (once, over the monthly ledger and at another time when a Parent was speaking to me about his girl!) I feel your gentle hands caress my breast and I can think of nothing but you.

Since I knew what we had done together — do you feel guilty? I do not, though I would have, had you been a Man — since I knew all we had done, I was wiser than Miss Vulpet when I established this school. My rules forbid intercourse of a private nature between both sexes. Only mischief and distraction can come of it. Of course I am rather indisposed to loving now. Losing you has done this to me! I suppose we must have marriage. But I have ghastly dreams of my sweet girls torn in childbed, their clean young flesh ravished and smutted by men. Well, it is God's will. Though really, Eustacia, I cannot understand why Paradise could not be peopled by wholly spiritual means.

My Seminary, being strict, has come to be called a "convent." My reputation is for absolute Puritanism. You will be amused, I daresay, by that. But since we parted, I have taken more and more seriously the mandate God gave me to educate my pupils for Eternity. Now I am in deep distress about the future, here and in the Beyond, of that young girl about whom I wrote you earlier.

She has been caught at night by the worst possible person — Miss Margaret Mann, who hates her — while entertaining the young woman to whom she was writing forbidden letters. Miss Mann, I may have told you before, is a rather humorless teacher of English, a poor minister's daughter. She has taken a great dislike to the girl, apparently because she won't take orders and writes with an annoying brilliancy. Miss Mann is Prefect of Corridors this month. She was about to retire when she noticed that the garden door rear was ajar. Endeavoring to close it, she overheard low conversation and followed the sounds to the girl's room, the door of which (supposed always to be left open!) was closed. Delighted to discover her in an infraction of the Rule, Miss Mann opened the door and found Emily — her name is Emily, that much I will tell you — on her knees before a handsome dark-haired young lady who seemed to be straining away from her slightly, though she was listening to what was being said to her. Their hands were clasped and a book, opened, lay between them. The book, which Miss Mann confiscated immediately, contained the sonnets of Shakespeare, for whom Emily has an inappropriate regard.

Of course, Miss Mann immediately came to me; I was compelled to go to Emily's room; and there I surveyed them both. They were very polite, but Eustacia, *they were like us!* They were not contrite, they did not feel guilty. Indeed, I do not think the dark-haired girl, whose name is Susan, could ever feel guilty about anything she did. She is perfectly self-possessed, perfectly sphinx-like, and somehow *mature* compared to young Emily. "We were merely reading, ma'am," she said calmly. "I have come to visit Squire Dickinson's daughter because of her bad cold and her father's concern about it. There was no time to ask for your permission, although the Squire would have wished you to give it."

Clever in the extreme, was that not? Perhaps she is aware that the Squire is among my chief benefactors! Eustacia, I daren't expel Emily, I need her father's support and I need the new patrons he has been bringing me. But I shall have to punish her and give out some reason for so doing. I cannot let anyone hear of the real reason. Perhaps I will say she has been too glib and careless in refusing to declare for Christ.

This "Sue" is, I think, a proud young chit. Emily clearly adores her. All you need do is look at her eyes. She will be made to suffer, as the one who loves best suffers. That is what happened between us. I could not please you.

Mary

$\mathcal{D}$ear Mr. Higginson,

You will think your last letter an absurdity when you read what I have to tell you here.

It is more than fifty years ago today that I caught Emily Dickinson not only in a lie but in an indecent act. I caught her with the woman who became her sister-in-law, alone in her bedroom with the door closed. What was going on behind those doors no right-living woman would ever speak of or be able to imagine. I was forced to report this to Miss Lyon, who was the soul of innocency and purity, and believe me, Mr. Higginson, I know that the shock of it shortened Miss Lyon's life. Only two years later, she was dead.

At first I had no intention of writing such things. But you have angered me with your foolish prating about Emily Dickinson's goodness! Apparently she was not just wicked when it came to men. She liked women, too. Or are you too noble to have heard about such doings? We live in 1892, Mr. Higginson. I, for one, *read*. I read the things that are printed in France, where they have prisons for such women as Emily Dickinson.

I remember that night very well. I was Patrol for the Corridors, a task I hated. Everyone was asleep. I could hear a dog barking over at the hotel, a dreary sound in the stillness. It seemed the very emblem of my life to me. While I walked, I was planning one of the verses I was writing; for I had taken to writing that spring very seriously. I admit that I was never able to write with much ease or swiftness. Your friend Miss Dickinson was just the opposite, even as a child. I envied her that.

I was traversing the corridor where the dutiful young ladies had said their prayers and were long since asleep. I remember — I am sorry to remember — that I had general feelings of envy that night. Laetitia Snowe was newly engaged, I recall, to a rich widower, a friend of her father's. The family had arranged her betrothal, but Letty was quite pleased about it and we had had a small collation of cake and mimosa wine to celebrate. No one asked Emily. It was well known that she was scared of weddings. As for me, I was chafing at my own situation. I hated my life as a teacher and saw no hope of any other.

As I walked along, I noticed with deep surprise that the door to the garden was not quite closed. Miss Lyon would have been most uneasy about that, and so I hurried to fasten the lock. Just then I heard voices: one, very intense and high and questioning, as Emily's always was, and the other, rather harsh and deep. The high voice was carrying on at a great rate while the lower one answered only in monosyllables. I knew the low voice could not belong to Emily Norcross, who was gone for the day. And I was very angry, for it was long after "Lights out." I made sure that the noise was coming from Emily Dickinson's room. It was.

I turned the handle of Emily's door and when it would not open, at first, I gathered my strength and flung it wide. And then I saw your New England nun, as you call her, locked in a deep embrace with another woman, who was seated by her side in the windowseat.

They were kissing on the lips! They were avid with each other. I was shocked to the very marrow of my bones.

"What are you *doing?*" I cried. Emily made me some exalted reply, but both were completely hardened against any sense of shame. I fetched Miss Lyon, who hurried to Emily's room immediately, separated the two girls, and conducted the interloper to the hotel. You may imagine my surprise when I discovered after the *Poems* came out that this bold girl called Sue had become Emily's sister-in-law, Mrs. Austin Dickinson! What kind of marriage could hers have been? What a fate for Emily's unsuspecting brother!

You say that Emily Dickinson hardly knew what Sin was. I think she knew what it was most intimately and that she embraced it from her youth. I think that among her sins were falsehood, theft, pride, blasphemy, and lust! But perhaps her major sin was indifference to all that her elders taught her was right. It is so long ago that I cannot remember how we punished her. I know that Miss Lyon did not punish her sufficiently because we needed the Dickinsons' money. Once again Emily's wealth protected her.

I suppose I shall not hear from you again, Mr. Higginson. So be it!

Margaret Mann

*Y*ou called me "Leopard," I guess because of my
spots: my freckles? my sins?

I call you "Cleopatra."

And this is the Wilderness.

But,

With thee, in the Desert —
Leopard breathed — at last!

Emily

$\mathcal{D}$ear Abiah,

You being Cousin Emily's old friend and (further-more) engaged to Reverend Strong, I take pen and seat myself to write to you about all that has befallen Cousin Emily here at Miss Mary Lyon's. I am in hopes, dear Abiah, that you might prevail upon my cousin to change her ways and join the Church.

Cousin Emily has been in partial disgrace with the faculty for some time — because she composes verse, reads at night, writes essays that are too original, steals food, wanders into the woods, talks back in English class, and commits many other infractions of the Rule. You are so good, you would never suppose her capable of them!

Now, however, she is in danger of expulsion, per-haps. I will describe for you what happened last night and you will see how serious an offender she is.

For some reason Miss Lyon announced late yester-day afternoon that she would have a last meeting with all girls who had not yet taken the oath to serve Christ and only Him forever. She ordered that those still with-out hope of being saved come at once to her rooms, where she would attempt to move their hearts one last time. Then, she said, we would all meet together in the great hall of the Seminary, where those saved would rise together and sing "Salvation by Grace" but those who were still without hope would be asked to retire to their rooms. She never actually used the word "expulsion."

But does she mean to cast out the remaining hard hearts? I feared that Emily Dickinson would be among them and she was.

I do not know about Miss Lyon's private meeting with the Hopeless. But the general meeting was as awe-provoking as anyone could wish. There were two preachers brought from South Hadley Village, and Miss Lyon preached herself on the subject of the Good Thief and how he was taken by Christ to be with Him in Paradise and how we should none of us want to be the Bad Thief, who went straight to Hell for not loving his Savior. All the time Miss Lyon was talking I watched Emily D. out of the side of my eye. While so many other girls were weeping, she was wearing her far-away look as if she knew other kingdoms where she would rather dwell.

At last, Miss Lyon asked all who wanted to be Christians and who believed in Christ as their only hope to rise. And do you know, Abiah, so great was her eloquence that everyone in the whole room rose. All save one! You may imagine my anguish when Miss Lyon left the dais and proceeded to where Emily Dickinson was sitting — right there in the front row, as if she had no cause to hide for shame.

"And you, Emily?" Miss Lyon asked softly.

"Had your words assumed a form to which I could assent, I would certainly have tried to please you, Miss Lyon," Emily said.

"You see this as a mere matter of words, Emily?" Miss Lyon said.

"Saint John calls Christ himself 'The Word.' Words are very important," Emily said.

She is packing her bags right now to go home. We do

not know whether Miss Lyon expelled her. Although I do not like my Cousin Emily — I cannot *like* what I cannot understand! — I will be honest. I am afraid of what my Uncle Edward may do. He is not used to disobedience. Emily loves my Uncle Edward and Aunt Emily, of course, and she doesn't seem to fear them any. (I still remember how happy she was when they suddenly came to see her here, about a month after she arrived. She was sitting at the window as she likes to, and when she perceived them, walking toward the Sem from the hotel, I thought she would die of satisfaction. "Do You Love Your Parents, Emily?!" she nearly shouted to me with glee. "Then you can understand my transport right now!" Another girl would just have said, "Oh, it's Mother and Father walking over from the hotel. I'm so glad!") Surely even her parents must know how peculiar Emily is. My mamma broke her habitual silence about these matters in a letter to me yesterday. In it, she said, "Your Cousin Emily has been a great mystery and surprise to my dear sister, as to us all." I have known for some time that she would not return here next year. But no one thought she would be expelled, if that is what has happened. Perhaps Miss Lyon has given up on her or perhaps she is merely sent home to reflect.

Could you not write to Emily, Abiah, and implore her to join the church and declare herself saved — even if she don't believe in *any* of it? (I certainly don't know if I do myself; but I would not want people to shun me.)

Remembering your visits to Monson, Abiah, with affection.

Yours sincerely,
Emily Norcross

$\mathcal{D}$ear Sue,

I have come home from Miss Lyon's to stay for a while. Whether I shall return, I do not know. I am tempted to stay forever.

You will not approve, for I know you love "Degree" and the title "Graduate" might seem to you worth lying for. But except when it comes to love — or when it is a question of Art (describing things as I *want* them to be for the effect!) — I cannot seem to lie.

Austin fetched me in the larger cabriolet with the curtains, so I knew that Father knew I did not wish to be seen. Indeed, I rarely wish to be *seen* if it means being found out as "different."

It is beautiful to be At Home. With her gentle smile, Mother divested me of my coat and said, "You have been away from this house much too long, Emily. The house misses you when you are gone." And it is true, dear Sue, that I feel the house preserves a sympathy with *me* in particular. The long, cool corridors, the high windows full of light, my "Northwest Passage" (as I call it) under the roof, where I can go to avoid the unwelcome guest — these make up my fortress. "In My Father's House there are many Mansions," Christ said. Well, this Mansion is adequate for me. The only other manse I would ever enter, Sue, is your own heart! I have not told you of my Northwest Passage: it is a little place, scarcely large enough for a mouse, but then I have a small size. Here I shall stay, in the castle that defends

me, its Queen! And here I shall become Something —
what, exactly, I do not know as yet.

I told Father of my loneliness at Miss Lyon's. She
never told Father about your visit, Sue. She wrote a
note to him, saying only that she feared my poor health
was keeping me from "taking Religion seriously." I
told Father that I *do* take religion seriously — seriously
enough not to embrace it. And do you know, Sue, Father actually laughed! I have never seen Father laugh.

He says I may stay home now for good, help with the
housework and maintain my education as I am able.
He was wearing his darkest frock coat on the day of our
interview in the formal parlor and the snow was falling
outside the window as he spoke. Everything about my
whole life seemed plain to me — black like his coat,
white like the snow — as if Father were not just a law-
yer but a Supreme Court Judge delivering a sentence:
the sentence upon my life! For a moment, only a moment, I was frightened. Then I felt relief, a flood of
ecstasy. Oh, Sue, I find Ecstasy in living — the mere
sense of living is joy enough! My heart is a flower, open
to the sun.

Now I have what I want, I can do as I please.

Do you know, Sue, Father said, "No Dickinson
should be forced to violate his conscience."

Now what do you think? I have begun a list of all the
subjects I wish to explore and everything I want to write
about. Thus far, here are the subjects:

> Whether or Not There Is Life after Death
> Whether Mr. Emerson Is Correct about
> the Look of the Morning Sky

How It Feels to Be the Frost
   (this will take imagining)
The Limits of Friendship
The Nature of Love
Deprivation: How It Stimulates the Fancy
Differences Between Men and Women
Food: Does the Body Feed the Soul
   or the Reverse?
The French Revolution
Snakes: Why Do People Fear Them?
Heaven: A Site Devised by the Mind
The Cardinal Virtues
Birds
The Final Journey: Is the Soul Conscious
   on the Road?
The Flowers and Their Special Meanings

and finally

   My Sue: All That She Hopes,
     All That She Thinks

But, Susie, Austin says you are going away! Where? And why have you not called on me when he told you I was at home?

One reason I *came* home was to be near *you*.

     Your
     Emily

$\mathcal{M}$y dear Mrs. Strong,

What a warm blaze of Memory your letter allowed me to bask in! How kind it was of you to write to me about Emily's poems. I remember her speaking of you long, long ago when she and I first became friends. As you say, you and she were warm correspondents for several years. (Along that line, I must tell you that she was rather hurt when you broke off the correspondence shortly before your marriage; but then Emily was always very vulnerable, as I myself was forced to learn.)

Yes, the poems are quite wonderful. If anyone should know that, it is I. Miss Lavinia gives out that it was due to *her* efforts that Mr. Higginson was willing to sponsor the publication of an unknown poet's work. Indeed, she is saying — and writing to newspapers, besides! — that after she had been "disappointed by her sister-in-law's refusal to find an editor" for Emily's poems, she turned to Mrs. Todd and Mr. Higginson, the present editors. Before writing further, I would wish you to know, Mrs. Strong, that I never precisely refused to act with respect to Emily's poetry. I was not very well in the 1880s. In 1883, I lost my little boy, the darling of all our hearts and a special favorite of his Aunt Emily. In 1886, Emily passed to her "Rendezvous with Light," as she wrote of my son Gilbert. Mr. Dickinson and I had an older child in uncertain health.

When Lavinia brought Emily's poems to me — she

found them in a locked box in Emily's room after the funeral, she had never guessed how many her sister had written! — I was in a sort of daze of distress or perhaps suppressed anger. My husband's "business" affairs kept him from giving me much comfort. I was always left quite alone. When I looked into the box and my eye fell on those exquisitely hand-written verses of Emily's, verses that brought me back in time to a better age when we were both young, when we were *true* neighbors and sisters (instead of residents of the same street), a time before she came to shun all company including my own, my heart sank in my breast! I could do nothing about the poems. I remember reading them to admiring friends at a dinner party once or twice. But even on those occasions, I felt I had done her an injury. Emily herself was private; she was a Soul Alone and Apart. Was I to be the one to lift her veil?

That she wrote the poems is enough.

It is I who best remember her writing them. I helped her with many, many of them, as the world does not realize (but no matter). Indeed, if Emily fancied herself a poet, I always knew that I was a poet too. There were a great many occasions when, as girls will, we wrote competitively. I would write a poem for Emily to imitate and she would do so. Her very best poems were written that way, as responses to my suggestions. Indeed, I wonder, Mrs. Strong, if you might not like to read some of *my* poems. Let me copy a few lines for you.

This is called "Amor." I wrote it in 1884 when I heard the harsh bluejay (of which Emily, too, so often writes) making love to his mate. If you like Emily's many poems about birds, you will like this one, and may see how identical our two geniuses were! My poem:

> A soft sweetness caught my ear,
> Unlike the other sweetness
> And putting by my prosy book
> I sought the bird that made this.
> Perchance a passenger bird
> Had stopped to win my heart
> Or cat-bird had gone mad
> And sung a human part.
> A bluejay sung unto his mate
> In cosy nest close by,
> The song their happy fate,
> The song the shining sky.

You may know Emily's poem "A bird came down the walk," in which she talks about the bird biting an angle-worm in half, drinking a dew from a convenient grass, and then unrolling his feathers to row himself home in a "plashless" sky like an ocean: it is very similar to my own thought! I was able to help her many times, I was able to make her change poems that I did not think worthy of her great gifts; and never have I revealed this to any human soul before!

You ask what she was "like" in later years when you were no longer friends. She was dazzling; her wit alone was dazzling. Her thoughts were rare and precious as old ivory. No one knew her as I knew her. It was I who dressed her body for its last sad journey — do you think the family would have asked me to do this, had they not known all that I meant to her? She was not ill until her very last years. It is true that she did not "cross her

Father's House to any house or town," as she put it, from about her thirty-third year. I save a letter of hers, keep it at my bedside, in which she says quite simply that she prefers wild buttercups to drawing-rooms. But she was not a mad spinster or New England nun or any of the rest of it that the reviewers say. For all her aristocratic birth, she was simply a solitary lover of Nature, and shy.

It wounds me that people imagine we were not friends at the end. We were somewhat estranged, perhaps, but then Emily had permitted a friendship, a relationship between herself and a woman who had done me great harm — the Mrs. Todd who helped Colonel Higginson with the *Poems*. It has been difficult for me to forgive Emily that! But we loved once, when we were little girls of seventeen. And the Past has a power . . .

You inquire about the fabled romance that Emily is supposed to have had with a married man. And you observe, Mrs. Strong, that you used to think she was rather afraid of men. The latter is not quite true. She had several intense friendships with men and much preferred their conversation (as indeed brilliant women often will, since the ladies so often insist upon confining their observations to children's clothes and recipes). I admit to having told a few persons — for Truth should out! — that there *was* a man, one man *only* whom Emily truly loved, early on in her life. But he was married and a father. Moreover, he was a minister, like your own husband. Had it been otherwise, we might have had the married woman Emily always feared to be, but no poems. She liked children, she was adorable with my own; but she was very afraid of giving birth. Is there any one of us honest women who is not? Were you not, Mrs. Strong? I told my sisters-in-law all I suffered with each of my children and it did not improve their zest to be married. Emily was never eager to be married. But she always wanted to be loved. She had flirtations. Some of them were quite robust. I will say no more.

I was moved by your confession to the effect that you found Emily's "intensity" disturbing when you were schoolmates. You can have no idea of my own experience in that regard. Both Emily and her brother, my husband, were what can only be called " passionate." On the one hand, it could be transporting to be in their company, you could be quite lifted out of yourself by their enthusiasms. Do you know what my daughter Martha said of Emily last evening? "She put more excitement into the event of a dead fly than her neighbors got from a journey by stage-coach to Boston." This was the Emily who made me think and feel so deeply about life. On the other hand, they were both — brother and sister — *needy*. They could devour the soul right out of your body, they could ask and ask and ask for a warmth, I would say a *heat*, that you could not for all your efforts produce! I failed my sister-in-law many times, but she asked of me too much.

I blush to be writing so openly to you, dear Mrs. Strong, but your letter moved me. I am getting on, too, now, nearly sixty-one. That seems to me very old indeed. So many of our friends are dead — Samuel Bowles, for example, who was at one point the dearest friend of all of us here, Emily included. (Although he formed a rather embarrassing habit of writing to me fondly, and coming to "Evergreens," my home, to see me, Sam also really liked Emily. He was one of the very few who did not, almost automatically, find her peculiar and plain.) I look up at the sunsets sometimes and wonder if they are both of them up there, somehow, where "the crimson children play in the West," as Emily described it.

I am happy that you admire her poems. If they survive into the next century, something of each of us will survive along with them. I send you cordial good wishes.

Susan Huntington Gilbert Dickinson

$\mathcal{D}$ear Miss Mann,

I am not one to dodge a challenge; and that is what the last line of your last letter constitutes!

Your letter is really a species of slander; I wonder if you know that.

Of course, I do not believe its implications are, any of them, true!

Nor do I believe that Miss Emily and Mrs. Austin "hated" each other at the end of Miss Emily's life. I feel I must tell you whatever I know about all this, if only to set the record straight. The truth is that Mrs. Austin had a habit of lying about Emily Dickinson, and about why she felt more comfortable out of the glare of Society. Mrs. Austin grew ashamed, I gather, of her sister-in-law's "eccentricities," as she called them. For Mrs. Austin was always concerned with "what people might think" and with preserving the lustre of the Dickinson name in western Massachusetts. The Honorable Squire Dickinson had been, you may recall, a member of the House of Representatives. His daughter-in-law was extremely proud of it, and very anxious to see his illustrious mantle draped about the shoulders of her older son "Ned," named for him.

People were whispering more than usual about Miss Emily's habits in the '60s — not only because of her reclusion, but because she took to gardening at twilight and because she began asking others to address the envelopes to her many letters. (When this is done in New England, as you know, people immediately think "A love affair!") In my small way, I tried to suppress all this gossip by urging Miss Dickinson to visit me in Boston. One appearance at my Circle for Literary Ladies and rumors of her misanthropy and hermeticism would die! However, with her accustomed modesty, she refused. About her nocturnal gardening, it seemed no use to point out to all the busybodies that Miss Emily had eye trouble, a tendency to inflammation of the iris that made being abroad in full sunlight painful. People thought it just another instance of her avoiding most society. They were wrong. She was sociable, but in her own selective way.

Now Mrs. Austin, of whom you write — without much real knowledge — fancies herself a poet. Certainly she is widely read. Her own richly romantic sensibility, combined with the desire to offer a credible excuse for Miss Emily's withdrawal, led her to make up a story about Miss Emily's hopeless love for a married minister. (For that is what she did.) This story was, and is, better known than any about Miss Dickinson and Judge Lord. As Mrs. Austin described it, Miss Emily renounced the world, dwelling alone in her chamber like an anchorite whose Lord was Love, hoping to be united with the minister in Heaven. Her fabrication implicated a wholly unsuspecting, firm friend of Miss Emily, with whom she was in correspondence — the Reverend Charles Wadsworth of Philadelphia. Reverend Wadsworth had been, Miss Emily told me before she died, her "Shepherd from little girlhood." She was horrified and outraged by this twisting of the truth.

And this was only one of many lies that Mrs. Austin spread about Miss Emily. But Miss Emily never "hated" her. She disapproved of her mendacity. In addition, she was often wounded by Mrs. Austin's caustic manner; for her sister-in-law could be condescending, as married women often are with maiden ladies, and as Mrs. Austin was with most persons anyhow. (I have always supposed that Miss Emily's poem "She dealt her pretty words like blades" was probably written after a conversation with Mrs. Austin!)

But, as for the story, the village relished it! The idea that one among them could have had so much probity as not to pursue, or permit the pursuit of, a man with a wife and children! That Emily Dickinson was living a recluse as a tribute to love — why, it made her a heroine, like Mary Scudder in *The Minister's Wooing*. Although in the obituary for Miss Emily, which she wrote for the newspapers, Mrs. Austin did not allude to the made-up romance, the legend of it lives on. I have all this from Mrs. Todd, who had it at first-hand from Miss Emily's brother. You see, Miss Mann, what imagination is capable of! I think you should learn to control your own.

The little tableau between Mrs. Austin and Miss Emily that you described to me was undoubtedly as free of any immodesty as the snow-white flowers with which I associate my dear friend. Miss Dickinson was very intense. I am certain that you misunderstood, and misunderstand, the significance of her behavior — if, indeed, you saw what you say you did! Mrs. Austin is by all accounts a cold-hearted person. "Avid" is a word that well describes her attitude to money, I take it, not people. In fact, since Emily Dickinson's poems were published to such acclaim, the chief interest she has shown in them is monetary. Possessing a few that were unknown to Mrs. Todd and myself, she has been trying to sell them to the magazines.

Mr. Austin Dickinson was so angered by his wife's behavior to his sister in later years that he would not allow Mrs. Todd and me to publish one of the loveliest of her juvenile poems that begins "One Sister have I in this house," and which was written for "Sue — forever-more."

Mrs. Todd has been much persecuted by Mrs. Austin. In this connection, I see no reason to conceal what you may already have heard. Mrs. Austin has taken it into her head to believe that her husband and Mrs. Todd have been more than friends. Being well acquainted with Mrs. Todd — who is perfectly devoted to *her* husband, Professor David Peck Todd — I find that impossible to believe. The story seems to be another all too evident fabrication of Mrs. Austin's. Miss Lavinia told me in confidence that she thought Mrs. Austin's cruelties shortened the poet's life. Now her cruelty persists, wounding others.

But I will say once more that I doubt Miss Emily ever "hated" anyone or anything. She was beyond it.

What seems to me most tragic is that so much pain and so much rancor — like your own, Miss Mann — should cloud the atmosphere that surrounds these splendid poems of my much-missed Friend.

You are right. I shall not reply to any more of your letters.

Sincerely,
T. W. Higginson

$\mathcal{D}$arling,

Love has but one date — the first of April, now and forevermore! Spring is a happiness so beautiful, so unique, so unexpected, that I don't know what to do with my heart. What do you advise? Could I give it to you?

When I think of you, my heart is on fire! I love you so, Sue, why do you never write to me or see me?

Thank you for the flowers, though — their tender smiles put me in mind of you.

Your
Emily

*L*ove has but one date, the first of April — now, and
forevermore!

> Adventure most unto
> itself
> The Soul condemned
> to be
> Attended by a single
> Hound
> Its own identity.

$\mathcal{D}$ear Emily,

Strange that you should have written to me about Emily D., for I had been thinking of her and how she has changed. She always seemed to me different. I never believed her when she said she had an interest in the fashions, for instance. You recall how she always turned herself out in brown like a dreary little bird. (But a sweet bird. Her smile was sweet.) She wrote to me once that she liked to "cut a timid caper." But it sounds as though her capers have gone beyond the usual dancing in hallways that she used to do at Amherst Academy, and reading novels under her desk in the arithmetic class. I don't think Emily cares for groups or institutions. Maybe she thinks Heaven will be full of too many folks for her liking and that's why she don't declare for Christ, lest she find herself there! Perhaps the Lord will take her anyway.

But Emily, I cannot write to her. You may not know it, but I am engaged to be married. My intended is a divinity student of sober temper who is displeased by Emily's letters to me. She takes so many liberties, she is funny about serious things and serious about the commonplace . . . well, Samuel don't know what to make of it and he has forbidden me to reply. He feels she is too set on my replying, as well.

Why should I write when our future paths will be so different anyhow? For who will marry her with all those words rushing from her mouth, and all her star-gazing? I fear she is doomed to nonentity while the rest of us, happy wives and mothers, achieve our immortality.

Yours,
Abiah Palmer Root
(soon to be *Strong*)

$\mathcal{D}$earest Millicent, our beloved daughter,

New Year's Day! For some reason known only to God, I sense that this year may be my last. And so I feel I must write something to you, Millicent, something that might at last excuse me and our lives — David's and mine — to you. I know what you think of us in your deepest heart, though you try to be loyal and conceal it. I have worried for *so* many years that to disapprove so much of your parents might make you ill in the end. For your grandparents, my own father and mother, I cherished nothing but the most loving respect. But of course, they were the souls of propriety, they did not challenge my youthful sensibilities as I know I did yours.

What you *must* believe is that I never planned it! My love for Austin Dickinson and his for me was an Act of God. It was a sacred thing, it had its own consecration. You know Emily's poems well, so you know how she writes about "Master" — that her passion for him was ordained throughout all eternity. Mine for Mr. Dickinson was the same. Despite Sue. Despite even your father, whom I continued to love in a different way, and who himself loved Austin. We might not have had our affair had your father forbidden it. He permitted it. He encouraged it. We were three people indifferent to commonplace attitudes and mores — even as Emily was. You once said you hated me for removing your father's wedding ring from my left hand and replacing it with a ring of Mr. Dickinson's; but he was my King, just as Emily wrote about that mysterious man of the love poems. I could do no less. In my passion for him, I seemed to be helpless. You are married now, so can't you understand? Some day, perhaps! But it pains me to think of the pain we gave you. I know that Austin's children, Mattie and Ned, insulted you continually, although he tried to stop them. That demon, Sue, wanted you to be wounded since anything and anyone to do with me, she hated.

But Millicent, *if you love me,* I beg you to take up what I abandoned and see to the further publication of Emily's poems. There are still so many in that box to be copied and edited. It was wrong of me to give up the task. I could not help it, I was so angry and hurt! After Austin died and Lavinia fought me in court to revoke his deed to me of that strip of land — land on which we might have had our own home! for your father could never give me a home, we were not prosperous — after Lavinia turned on me when I did *just what she asked,* when I had spent *years* with those home-made manuscripts of Emily's, deciphering her difficult handwriting, rectifying her punctuation, regularizing her crazy rhymes, typing and typing and typing on that primitive machine, copying them all clearly and changing some of the words to make sense of the poems! And after I had written to Colonel Higginson, begging him to be Emily's sponsor and find a publisher and help me select which poems would be safest to bring before the public! And after I had given lectures to ladies' clubs and libraries, explaining the poems and making Emily's success even more spectacular than it was — for, as you know, Millicent, it was through my efforts chiefly that Emily's *Poems* became a best-seller: I gave Lavinia the proceeds, too, which was only just, since she was Emily's heir and it was the first money of her very own that Lavinia Dickinson had ever had. After I had done all that, to have her turn on me! She — and Emily too! — *knew* what Austin was to me, and all I had been to him. He wanted to die, he told them both, before he met me, so miserable was he with Sue. Lavinia proved she understood all that, because she persuaded Ned to admit me secretly to the Evergreens on the day of Austin's funeral so that I might kiss his dear face in the coffin without Sue's knowledge. She hated her husband, yet she was upstairs when I arrived, adorning herself in expensive mourning! But Lavinia turned on me, when it came to the deed of gift. Land was more important to her than friendship. Or honor. After that, I could not go on. I wanted nothing more to do with any of the Dickinsons.

But I was wrong.

Emily's poems are wonderful — more wonderful than I realized even in the beginning, when their haunting, compelling effect on me was more intense than I could ever express. After Austin died, they were the only thing except my duty to you that kept me sane. There are still a great number of poems that make up her "letter to the world," which the world has not seen. You must copy them and have them published! Don't let Mattie Dickinson, that vicious woman's vicious daughter, beat you to it! Sue had copies of some of the poems Emily wrote down by hand in what I call those "fascicles" of hers. (You know what they look like — small, rudely made booklets composed of letter paper sewn together with twine, in which she carefully inscribed her heart's profoundest sentiments. I have shown them to you so often. As a child, you used to turn their pages over with your chubby fingers and gaze at them wonderingly and try to dislodge the strings.) When the *Poems* came out, Sue was jealous of what I had done to establish Emily as a writer. She thought that, because of their early friendship, she *owned* her husband's sister. Furthermore, she was avaricious. Anything for money! So she tried to publish some of the poems in her possession that had been jotted down by Emily on little pieces of household stationery, bargain fliers, recipe pages. Emily had a habit of sending Sue poems after she wrote them. Poor Emily, she was so innocent, she never knew how venal that "Sister" of hers really was, and she was always loyal to the past! Memory with its "cedar feet" shod in "adamant" — that is how her line goes, I think.

You remember when Sue finally died — 1913 — and how almost immediately thereafter, Mattie brought out a collection to rival mine. *The Single Hound*, she called it, after that poem about living alone that seems to explain Emily's fate and nature. But what a shabby affair Mattie's book is, and how full of mistakes! She can't tell the difference between *seal* and *sail*. When I change Emily's language, it's to improve it, not because I lack patience to decipher her writing! Mattie has no interest in Emily's poems. She fancies, as Sue did earlier, that *she's* a better poet than Emily ever was! What a blind, ignorant pair they are.

I myself, as you well know, cherished literary ambitions. From the very first, taking on Emily's poems meant the sacrifice of my own hopes and dreams. I did it for Austin.

No. That is not quite true. I also did it for *her*. For Emily. When your father and I moved to Amherst, and Sue and Austin took us up and made much of us, I had no interest in Emily. But then the townspeople began whispering to me about Squire Austin Dickinson's strange sister, who sent sick people gifts of fruit and flowers with poems buried in the center of a rose or a grape cluster, poems so beautiful and uncommon that they thought about them for days. I wanted to meet her.

To my great disappointment, I never did. Emily was growing frail then, so she rarely left her bedroom. But I used to walk from our little home in the dell over to the great Dickinson house in the twilight and I would play the piano for Emily as she sat in her room upstairs. I would often play Chopin, the silver chords shimmering in the dusk — Emily was unfamiliar with Liszt and Chopin, but positively enraptured by their music. Her own education and training had been in Mozart, Bach, and the earlier composers. And she was *thrilled* by my playing of Chopin. I always hoped that she would suddenly appear in her ghostly way in the parlor doorway and that then we would share a moment of communion between two artistic natures! It never happened.

But I was conscious of her gratitude to me and I knew we were friends. She would often send me in a glass of sherry on a silver salver, or one special rose from her garden. Marks of her gratitude, as if she knew what lay ahead: that I would be the one who carried her name into the future, the one who secured her fame. I realized that she had chosen me. I knew that she entirely sanctioned my love for Austin!

How, then, could I refuse to edit the poems when I was asked to do so?

Still, it was not Emily but the same Lavinia who later betrayed us that made the request. I can see Vinnie now, waiting at the door of the little cottage the College gave your father and me when he became Professor of Astronomy — that sweet but oh so small cottage. (Did I tell you all this? I can't remember.) It was about two years after Emily died and late at night. By that time, Lavinia had taken to staying in the house and coming out only in the evening, just like Emily. She was wearing one of her weird outfits — that rusty red shawl with the purple skirt and the yellow shoes. Her fuzzy gray hair was falling into her eyes, and she was carrying a heavy box, full of those manuscripts over which I was to labor so long!

I knew what she was working up to, because I knew that, at first, after she found them in Emily's bedroom, she had given the manuscripts to "Old Scratch," as Austin and I sometimes called Sue. And I knew that Sue had done absolutely nothing to get them published. (Why Vinnie would have chosen Sue in the first place is quite beyond my comprehension, for by the time Emily died, Vinnie and Sue were not close.) Well, Destiny may have forced me to come into Austin's life after Sue. But I vowed I would not come a poor second to her as editor of the poems! So, as soon as Vinnie began to lament that Sue was more interested in giving parties and going to Europe than in readying her sister-in-law's poetry for publication, I said simply, "Don't turn to me, Vinnie, if that's what you're doing. I have a husband. I have a little girl. I have my painting-on-china and my essays on the flowers of Amherst. I haven't the time."

Then Miss Lavinia Dickinson, daughter of the proud old Squire, sank to her knees and with tears streaming down her withered old face, she cried "But you *must* help! Oh please, dear friend, *these are Emily's poems!*" Had she said "This is Christ the Lord," she could not have been more vehement.

What could I do, Millicent? I obliged her, though the intense amount of work I was forced to do over the years compromised my health, spoiled the serenity of your childhood, and wrecked my chances to be a writer myself. I might have been famous! And then she betrayed me.

I am convinced now, however, that we must try to forget all this. We must remember our duty to Emily's poems. We cannot count on Mattie Dickinson to do justice to her aunt's reputation. Love asks this — not just my love for Austin but my devotion to Emily. Please do not fail me, Millicent. If you will do this one last thing for me, you will be richly blessed, I know. Your poor father would have wished it, too. Perhaps he *was* very broken at the end and I still cannot bear to think of him in that dreadful asylum. But he never quite abandoned his loyalty to Austin and me. And he admired Emily's poetry.

I will put this letter in the vault and should I not see the year out, you will find it. You will read it, and I hope you will act on it. Although Emily's popularity has waned somewhat since those early volumes of the '90s, there will always be people who value her verse. They may as well have what remains of it.

Remember, dear girl, that I have always loved you!

Mother

*M*y dear Clarissa,

It is scarcely a week since Emily's death, but you cannot imagine my terrible loneliness! I don't think anyone could. I am at a loss to describe it! For ever since we were little girls, Emily and I have been so dear to one another. Perhaps you never knew it, for I am sure that it is not generally known in the family, but the reason that we never — either of us — accepted a suitor was that we could not bear to be parted. "I could not imagine caring for anyone as much as I care for you, Vinnie," Emily often told me. But now we *have* been parted — by cruel Death, and I struggle on here, trying to find a reason why I myself should be living.

You see, when Emily was with me, I *did* have a reason. You know how gentle and sweet and discriminating and lady-like she was. Mr. Bowles used to say that she was like an angel or like one of her own orchids — or, as I often thought, not too different on the surface, anyway, from the fragile, frothy cakes she baked. The most elegant cakes full of nourishment and yet so delicate! She was fastidious and shy and so she needed *me*, a Tartar with a ready tongue, who was not afraid to answer doors and speak sharply to tradesmen and keep off callers if Emily was busy. Emily was *always* busy. Whenever anyone asked me about our family I said that Father believed, Mother loved, Austin had Amherst to build up, and Emily had to think. That was *her* business. Indeed, she told me once, "My Business Is 'Circumference,'" Mr. Emerson's word. And I thought that by "circumference" she meant all her studying; for she was always keeping up her education, reading and reading just everything she could get her hands on — *Middlemarch* one moment and *Godey's Lady's* the next — so she could find things out. She'd go through the newspapers and magazines and clip advertisements, and Austin would buy the books for her, or, for a while, she borrowed Sue's. But yesterday, Clary, I learned that by "circumference" she didn't mean study. I will come to all that in a minute. What I have to tell here will shock and stun you as it did me. But my heart is too full just now to say it right off. First I need to give my wounds a voice. Do listen to me for a while, dear patient Girl as you are!

I am writing this at Emily's little desk by the window. When she wrote her verses, she sat here. It is sacrilege, perhaps, for me to use Emily's desk; but it brings me close to her. I have been here in her room all day, sorting her things to see which should be kept and what given away. Just now I look lovingly at her garnet brooch. You won't recall it for she hardly ever wore it, she disliked jewelry, but Father gave it her and so she valued it. I have next to me the little gold ring with "Phil." — for his middle name of Phillips — on it from Judge Lord. Except for her books and pictures, she had very few possessions. I am her heir, but I need nothing to recall her to me. She is everywhere, the house is rich with her, it is a shrine to her beautiful nature, even now! And I cannot imagine that ever being different. This will always be Emily Dickinson's House.

The morning after that sad walk to the burial, I was positively sick, Clary. I could not begin this task of sorting and the more painful one — destroying. But today, before sunset, I *must* put her personal letters in the fire. Our New England custom. Oh, Clary, it is sad to burn so many letters! She kept hundreds of them, all bound up with different colored ribbons and stacked in that antique chest of Mother's that carried her trousseau linens from Monson to Amherst when she married Father. You may remember it. There's a goodly pile from Helen Hunt, Mrs. Jackson that now is. Helen may be famous today for *Ramona*, but you and I knew her when she was just another girl from Amherst. Helen was always asking to visit here, Emily fascinated her, and she would suddenly arrive at our door and lumber out of her coach like a miniature ox, toting a leather briefcase all distended with long poems. She was always urging Emily to publish. Emily finally told me that with a sigh. Of course Emily wrote poetry so differently from Mrs. Jackson's way, but still Helen appreciated it. "You are a great poet," she would remark, and then my sister would smile in her rather sad and private manner. "What are you thinking at this moment, Emily?" I would always long to ask but I never did. I always respected Emily's privacy.

I've found letters from Sue before she married. My sister has bound *them* together with black ribbon and I think I know why: black for mourning. You, Clarissa, will comprehend some of Emily's feelings there. I was almost glad you could not come to the funeral; for you would have had to look across at the Evergreens, where Madame Susan made you suffer so painfully when she and Austin were your guardians. Emily and I never understood how Sue could forget that she herself had once been in the same position — without parents, living in another's home, though without the money *you* generously brought them, and she spent! It won't be hard to destroy Sue's schoolgirl letters, for they are practically ashes now. Emily must have read them frequently. She still loved Sue — it was her charitable soul that allowed it — even when Sue would send Emily the most terrible withering, blighting messages that always made her catch her breath and grope for a chair. "Never mind, Vinnie," Emily would say patiently. "She cannot help it. She has never known how to love." I was forced to allow Sue to do something before the funeral. I *hated* the idea and will tell you about it in a minute, but the only reason I did so was because I remembered my sister's loyalty.

The letters from our beloved Mr. Samuel are all tied in red satin ribbon. Those, I did not open, nor the ones from Judge Lord. The latter I will keep but never read. They are "hallowed ground." Mr. Samuel's widow, though, has already sent me a note by Sam, Jr., asking for Mr. Bowles's letters back. She says she will be more than happy to burn them for me herself. Also bound in red are some letters to a person called "Master." Those, I *did* cast my eye over, for of course Emily never knew anybody called by that name. They were surely not written for any living person. They were fantasies, I think, about some slave girl, like the concubine of Abraham. Or maybe she was imagining one of those old books we read as children such as *Jane Eyre*, where the governess loves "Master." Emily liked her mental games. These I won't burn either, for they are only literary.

Still before me, Clary, is telling you the great Secret of our House, and yet before I do I *must* relieve my grief a little more!

I pray you never know the sadness of parting from your sister. When I first entered Emily's room where she had slept since we were girls, thoughts came to me too deep for tears. I remembered being just a tot in the strange, misshapen baby clothes Mother dressed us in — Mother was awkward in almost everything, including dressmaking — and having Emily poke her head in my bedroom door, and say "Vinnie, get up now! In the matter of raiment you are greatly necessary to me." She wanted me to fasten her buttons! I recall I was simply *charmed* by how she put her request, and I mumbled over and over to myself for hours afterward "in the manner of rayment," thinking Emily meant that I was a reflection of her, a beam from her light. In many ways I was, all our days. She was maybe seven then; and that rare way in which she spoke was hers for as long as I can recall. To me, she was the Book of Revelation. Of course, by the end, I became *very* necessary to her as to clothes! You well remember, Clary, how she had all her dresses fitted on me. (All except one! The white robe you made for her that became her shroud.) She had come so much to dislike the intrusions of strangers, even our nice dressmaker Mrs. Henderson. Except for visiting with a child — you well know, everybody did, that she was always ready to run and play and chat with a child — she'd flee immediately if so much as the postman came to the door. Why that came about,

I don't know. I guess it was just a happen. So since she wouldn't let the dressmaker see her or touch her, I had to keep trim so that her dresses, all in white — not like mine, bottle green and black to hide the housecleaning dirt — would not be too large. I never minded, no more than I minded holding her hand when it thundered. Emily's "peculiarities," as our "Sister" Sue called them, were to me precious blooms from God's garden.

And she was grateful. Oh, Clary, you cannot know how my heart swelled when I read one of the letters she wrote to a friend. He sent it to me for a comfort. "Your bond to your brother," she said, "reminds me of mine to my sister — early, earnest, indissoluble. Without her, life were fear, and Paradise a cowardice, except for her inciting voice."

Yes, I have a loud voice! And I always used it to protect Emily. Oh, she made fun of me sometimes, I know. It didn't surprise me when you told me a few things she said. She could make people into caricatures, if she wanted. My spring cleaning always afflicted her. She didn't like her things disturbed. You couldn't get in to dust her room, so much was always going on in it — all those letters, and her indoor gardening: trowels! newspaper with seedlings on it! dirt! After all, she had the Conservatory, built just for her. "Why do you have to grow things in the bedroom, Emily?" I would say to her. But they were like her babies, the flowers, she had to have them by her. Whenever I housecleaned, she called me "Soldier," and "vicious as Saul" but we never really quarreled. We were different, yes, but like different birds in one nest.

Do not worry, I understood perfectly why you could not take the long journey to the funeral. But I do assure you, Clary, it was beautiful and just as Emily desired it. She had given Austin and me some little instructions — oh very few, and so timidly — and we followed them. As you know, she was weak for three years. It started with her grief over our nephew Gilbert's death and one day, when she was baking, we found her, fainted, on the kitchen floor. The doctor said it was "revenge of the nerves," all the strain from Judge Lord's passing as well as Gilbert's. Emily was more keenly sensitive than any of us, though Austin is also given to fits of anxiety now and they worry me.

After the first attack, she tried to go about as usual for almost two years. She was only bedridden in the last six months. She would read or write letters on her lap in that little sleigh bed of our Grandmother's, looking out her window at the trees and the change of seasons, as she always liked to do. Dr. Bigelow came often in the last weeks, but there was no help for her. She was very dizzy and feeble and terrified us by fainting again four or five times. The last time, we found it hard to call her back. After that, she lay down and never got up again. She had an embarrassing ailment, an infection in her kidneys, and maybe that was why she refused the doctor for so many months. At last Austin persuaded her to let good, puzzled Dr. Bigelow come a last time. He gave her quinine and belladonna, but to no avail. Of course it's a wonder he was agreeable to coming at all. Months before, when he first called, Emily wouldn't let him touch her. She paraded past an open door at a distance of about half a mile from where he was standing, with her face turned away. That was how she expected him to make a diagnosis! And really I was very angry with her for the first time in our lives. Dr. Bigelow complained later that the only disease you could detect under those conditions was mumps.

I remember her last day with horror — how long it seemed, how ragged her breathing was, and how Austin sat with me and held my hand and then said, when the six o'clock whistle was just sounding, "She's gone to the other side, Vinnie." She had written so many poems about it, and finally it had happened!

Emily and I spoke often of Death, so it seemed nothing unusual when she told me a few weeks before she felt the "difference" coming, that she wanted to be buried from the house and laid beside Father and Mother. She wished our Irish menservants to carry her by hand. She disliked what she always called the "Dark Parade" of undertaker's carriages (from her window she had watched it many times) and she wanted everything simple. She asked that the men go to the cemetery on the diagonal, not straight. That way, if the person lying in the coffin could see, she would always be able to see our house until the very last moment when the ground was shoveled over her. Emily loved this house. She said it was her "kingdom."

We invited a very few people, some of them distinguished — our minister and the President of the College among them — to the little service Colonel Higginson conducted in the parlor. There we brought Emily's coffin, and there her sweet face (so often hidden from prying eyes!) was briefly "on view." I debated whether it was right to show her off like that, but Austin desired it. Some of the townspeople had begun to speak of her as an eccentric who hid herself away because she was deformed. He wanted the neighbors who were invited to know how lovely she was. Colonel Higginson told me he thought she looked no more than thirty, with "perfect peace on her beautiful brow." I arranged pink cypripediums at her throat. The day was very warm, so the flesh was darkening there already. *How* it hurt me to see it! You know how Emily loved her cypripedium orchids. She said the name came from "Cyprus" and the flower stood for Venus, for love. As to love, I tucked two heliotropes in her hand to take to Judge Lord. Now they are together in Paradise.

After a while, we made a circle in the parlor around the coffin and Colonel Higginson read Emily Brontë's "Immortality Ode." That would have pleased her, for, like Mr. Bowles, Emily worshipped the Brontës. I could hear the birds singing outside, all her birds that were her favorites, and when we followed her little white coffin (I chose white, white is for children, and she was innocent as children) through the screen door at the back of the house, the bees were all buzzing around the hollyhocks, as they do in her poetry! The walk to the cemetery was the longest walk of my life, through the fields full of buttercups. *How* could they grow, and she not able to see them? Her final resting place was lined with pine boughs and violets. There were butterflies in the air all around, which she would have liked, and she is right alongside Mother and Father, which will comfort her. But oh, Clary, it broke my Heart when they lowered her so far down. I wanted to be at home with her again in our dining room with the applesauce loaf cooling on Mother's Spode charger and "Irish Maggie" pouring our tea and our fond conversation!

Sue, if you can imagine it, did not attend. Austin came in the company of Professor Todd's wife, Mabel. Yet Sue did not. And now I must confess to you that I allowed Sue to dress Emily for her last journey and compose Emily's obituary. As to the last, all right — she has, I admit, more acquaintance with Emily's poetry than Austin and I do. Emily sent so much of it to her. (I used to tell my sister, "*Why* do you try to impress her? It's not anything written but a bank cheque she'd want.") But when Sue begged me to let her wash and comb and dress my sister, my heart cried, That is *my* right. I permitted it, Clary, because to tell you the truth I am afraid of Sue. She can be violent, and I am alone now. Emily is not here to protect me. She was up in Emily's room a long while and I heard her sobbing when I stood outside the door. There will never be any figuring out of Sue.

But now I come to the great Mystery, the great Triumph, the dreadful Challenge. While I was searching for the letters, Clarissa, I opened Emily's cedarwood chest. In it was a locked box. Emily never locked anything against me in her life. Her door and heart were always open to me if I knocked. I could not understand why she locked this box. In the house were just the two of us, and she trusted the servants. Well, then I decided she had locked it against Austin, who was not above rummaging round. He owns the house, as you know, and he uses it as his. I went down to the pantry and got a wrench and, though I felt guilty — *when* did I ever disturb Emily's privacy? — I worked the box open. What I discovered astounded me, Clary. And it will astound you.

We all knew Emily wrote poems and we were proud, were we not? But Clary, she had written *hundreds* of poems. What I found in the box were forty little books, hand-sewn together, and in them all copied neatly above seven hundred verses. Some, I recognized and her hand I recognized as belonging to her penmanship of the sixties. No letters standing frozen and lonely like watchmen as they did lately, but her running hand — romantic and dramatic and, to me, like a brilliant song. Oh, Clarissa, what store she must have set by those poems, to have copied them so carefully, even with asterisks next to words she couldn't make up her mind about and other choices for them at the page bottoms. But she lost her courage, I think, because the booklets stop with that sixties handwriting! In the chest were many many other verses, scribbled on recipes and advertisements and bargain fliers from the Main Street stores, but she hadn't put them in any kind of order at all. Before the day was done, I found more poems — shoved among her clothes, tucked into her drawers, laid into her books, like stars obscured.

What fills me with an amount of guilt I can never convey to you is the fact that, close to her as I was, I never realized what Emily was doing! Why, she must have been writing every minute we left her alone, practically; for there are over a thousand poems I've found so far and I'm not finished looking. She must have been writing when she was tired out from cooking and from nursing Mother and during all those years when I fancied something was troubling her, something to do with either Sue or another person. . . . Something.

Since that is the case, I am determined to bring my sister's life work before the world. Read this poem! Consider its wisdom. And then tell me I'm wrong, if you dare!

> The Brain — is wider than the Sky —
> For — put them side by side —
> The one the other will contain
> With ease — and You — beside —
>
> The Brain is deeper than the Sea —
> For — hold them — Blue to Blue —
> The One the Other will absorb —
> As Sponges — Buckets — do —
>
> The Brain is just the Weight of God —
> For — Heft them — Pound for Pound —
> And they will differ — if they do —
> As Syllable from Sound —

What was *I* doing, I wonder, on the day she wrote that? Tending to all my pussy-cats, no doubt. I wish I had asked her how she felt about writing all those poems. But I loved her, that was all. In a way, her being a poet meant nothing at all to me. She was my *sister.*

Now I must rectify all that, all my neglect and obtuseness. I will have Emily's poems published! Sue will offer to help me, if she hears. But Sue I do not trust. It would be quite like her to change Emily's language if she chose or to do something glittering and false in their connection — something Emily would not like. Yet Sue did entertain Mr. Emerson once. Sue is literary.

You wrote to me most kindly, Clary, during Emily's last days, and it was dear of you to say that you thought I, too, had a poet's voice. Those little "poems" of mine in girlhood were just trifles.

There was never any poet in this family but Emily.

I miss her so!

Heartily,
Cousin Lavinia

*D*ear Emily,

I am here in Geneva, teaching as a pupil-teacher in the school not far from my sister's home. You will recall that this was my intention — to find a position teaching that would free me of Brother Cutler's dole as soon as possible. Perhaps Austin shall have told you by now where I am. He visited me last weekend.

Dear Emily, I hope we may be friends indeed, as you do; but it must be as two sisters. I know you are fond of me. It is a compliment. I shall always endeavor to suit you, especially in the matter of reading your poetry and giving you my opinion — or my applause, which is, I think, what you *really* crave. But as for writing of love . . . it is Austin who must do that. We have been speaking of marriage.

You know that I am proud and I am not sure that I can really love as he would wish it. But I mean to try. I want a home, dear Emily, a home such as you have always had, to which I may bring my family. You would not understand.

I hope you will be gracious if I marry your brother.

Susan

*M*aster,

I cannot write. My sight has fled in Visions. My hand is too nerveless to hold the pen. You know it —

Thank you for the Voice that came to me in the mornings, resonant with Mystery. You showed me the Word —

It is forty years now since that first day you visited me in white. My door was locked as it always is whenever I can lock it. Behind the Closed Door is every vista, all Romance — Like the risen Lord, you passed through the door and stood before me. Baffling you were and terrible and godly — Older than Time and younger than the Angels or the newest lamb in my father's field. My Life was mine no longer. You assaulted me, you ravished Me, I could not tell where my being vanished and yours began; and that is passion. Oh, Master, that is Love!

For a while, I feared that you had entered but would depart, never to come to me again! There have been those I loved who found it better to depart. My hands have been full many times, full to the finger-tips with the roses of Affection. But flowers from such gardens as I tend are neither francs nor furs, and She, for instance — Sue, you remember — would not receive them. You are different, Master. I think you have desired me for the very Soul-shine of me, for the mere Skeleton on which you hung your own flesh — You taught me the Word —

Do you recall our fond meetings when I was a schoolgirl at Miss Mary Lyon's? Ah, Master, do you recall how diligently I tried to give Miss Margaret Mann and the rest all they wanted and how you chided me until I stopped and agreed that I was Yours and could speak only as you intended? They thought me frivolous, they thought me disobedient, but I was only keeping the Counsel of my Lord. Some have thought me worse than disobedient. I am set down as strange and even lost, Master. I have known the Abyss for my love of You! My Christ, who puts out Christ's Face. My Love, who scatters other loves like armies!

Perhaps you will lead me home. I fear Extinction but could not placate the gods who annul it! Where shall I find myself tomorrow? In what Hovel of air will my soul have refuge? I think I shall be an island of Grass whom none but Beetles know! Fiery Lad of Earnest Heart, Keats thought his name was "writ in water." Mine is my father's: "E. Dickinson." But Father's will live — Men are marble monuments, and Women, the dust that slips between the fingers. My name goes into the Ground with the violets, yet theirs is no ignominious Fellowship —

Why did you enter, Master, why did you kindle in me the Zeal to light the Flame and then keep every man from reading its light? No one knows I am a poet but Mrs. Jackson, kind Helen of Colorado with her sonnets like sofa cushions and her ampler frame — My Sue had hopes of me once! She had hunger for Renown on my behalf, for Fame, that shifting food upon a fickle Plate. But not for me did she wish it — Cosmopolites with their emerald rings, their crowns and gowns, must be surrounded by personages of Import. I was to be an Earl for her. But Sue has not seen the Heart of my words these twenty years. I have stood at her Door and knocked, yet she has never opened — Still, there was the Girl she was, winsome, clear, and bright. My Pseudo-Sister. My Cleopatra, coarse and cruel. My comrade in the dimpled War in which we both were slain. She loves and hates me. I see it —

No matter. I had You, who took me for the very Soul-shine of me, nothing more. I got up in the morning to watch the road outside Father's gates, to wait for the grim white horse with the flashing hoofs and airy mane; and for the noble Rider, who covered me with caresses — who brought me the Sign! Years went by — your steady coming. I sat calmly through the long spun-out nights with the clock ticking and the cascading moonlight on the sill and the dance of the fireflies in the garden. Whenever you did not come, I swept my Heart and adorned it all the more for You! Like Psyche, I have seen Your Face. And now I cannot see —

Master, I am weary. The dyings have been too deep for me. First, Father's death; his heart was pure and terrible, I think there was none like it. I loved him and he never knew. I was not Austin to him — Then Mother, tender, timid bird-sprite, took her way into the Light. We never loved when we were mother and child. I was not Austin to her. But in her going, when I became her nurse, *her* mother, the Love came — the Diamond-shower that surprises!

I have known Cupid's darts, I have been no Stranger to the little god with epaulettes — It was not, as she imagines, only Sue I loved! You may recall your rival for a time, Mr. Bowles, who published the *Republican*. In his way he served you. But he never thought his "Queen" — that is how he used to name me; I hear his deep voice calling up the stair — ever really knew you. He never read a verse of mine he did not call — so condescendingly! — a "little Gem." Ah, the bullying, shaming patronage of Fondness! Mr. Bowles admired my verse the way a man commends the antics of his Dog, and it gashed me like the knife that cuts the Wound in the very Bread! He thought I was an interesting Woman. Nothing more. Well, he called me an "Angel" once — you may remember that scene in the drawing-room. I was in his lap, he had drawn me to Him — and when I arose suddenly, he said "and a Devil too." Mr. Bowles *liked* Women. In his deep purple Eyes, I was a Woman, with fluent hair like Rubies and a bosom . . . It seemed strange to me.

Mr. Samuel Bowles. I spent nights of imagined rapture in my life with Samuel Bowles. My Resurrection, my Eden: Mr. Bowles. Like Abiah of old, I have had *my* Samuel. He gave me what Sue always thought me too homely to have. And he spent a night once in my House. Dead these many years! Go thy great way, I feel thine eyes shining on me from Paradise! Thine eyes like comets. We will be together there, Mr. Bowles and I, as I have written. It amused me, Master, that he was married. You let me be "married" to him without the dangerous Swoon that seals a woman's life.

I never told you, Master — I refused Judge Lord

because I could not leave this room where you had visited me — You had ceased to visit me so often as before, do you remember? I stood at the window in the morning, just as I had in those days of the Civil War in my soul when you came to me constantly and my heart was full of you. But you rarely came. So I could not go to Judge Lord, for I knew you would not find the way there. I never told you adequately of my love and yet you have always known it. You always knew everything, from the first moment at the Gate. In our deepest delights, there is a solemn Shyness. All others were mere shadows of your Grace.

But vivid shadows: my orchids, my dog Carlo, my Sue!

Sue — I saw her some days ago, I think it was, for the first time in years. Hearing from a passerby that I was dying, she brought me some *crème brûlée* to give me strength on the road to the Cemetery. She brought me some custard to carry up to God. She was wearing her furs and diamonds, although it is very warm now in May and mine is an almost vacant Room. She has become all I feared she might.

You will come for me, Master, in the Coachless Coach, will you not, to escort me on the day I ride — you, who rode with me before, so many years ago, when I went to school? Sue came with Austin, the dark man with the money-bags who stole her from me so long ago, the man she tried to kill once, I am told. With a carving-knife. Yes, that would be her way. That was how she dealt her pretty words — "like blades." I would have died to make her mine before I knew I really was *your* Bride. Sue has fathomless eyes and a heart of stone! Vinnie heard her say she "gave" me my poems — that I merely copied her ideas, her words — Oh, Sue, Truth may be bald and cold, but it's good health and Safety, and the Sky! Lies kill. She has written with an insipid pen ever since she became a Woman. Austin is time-worn. "Mine Enemy is growing old," I said, "I have at last Revenge." No Revenge. Only happiness and the silence of a soundless Life. . . .

Austin's blooming young mistress, Mrs. Todd, sits downstairs in her ribbons and garters — playing the piano to me in the gathering Dark. She thinks I approve of her. She thinks I am her Friend. They kiss and writhe together in Mother's dining room with the doors locked and the Servants alert. But Passion cannot be quelled by Injunction, that is true. It possesses the Ultimate Power, the power which belongs to Ubiquity. To take their draught of Life will cost them precisely an existence. And all this must be a matter of indifference to me now! The bonny mistress painted a few Indian pipes "For Miss Emily, your favorite flower." I studied them. Education in drawing has declined since I was a girl at Miss Mary Lyon's. But what is education — is it Love?

Sue imagines I approve of Mabel and Austin's affair. *There* is a strange Revenge! Poor Sue has lost Gilbert. Will I see him where I tend — in that vast Sky of emptiness — or starburst — where I am going? The Boundlessness of that tiny boy dwarfs Heaven and Hell. Oh, matchless Earth: we underrate the chance to dwell in thee! Dim is the heavenly Prospect beside thee — Glory is here below. Yet the Dead are not dissuaders but lures — Keepers of that great Romance still to us foreclosed. Grace is still a secret. That they have all existed none can take away.

Death, whose "If" is everlasting —

Are not all Facts Dreams as soon as we put them behind us? This room is now a dream. My shawl. The white dresses I wore to match your robes. My garnets and Snood — the adornments of elderly Spinsters. The apple-tree outside the darkening window and in the stillness, the blue fly that keeps buzzing as I drift, soundless —

I think it will be Vinnie who discovers the poems where I have hidden them. Loyal, invincible Vinnie! Austin, also my dear but my rival, will never want them published. Sue will be jealous of them, and she will be afraid to have the love poems linked to her. She presumes that they are all for her, Elegant Fantasist! But some are for Mr. Samuel and most are for You! Death clears the darkest dream. What will become of the poems, I wonder? Vinnie may burn them to protect my Privacy. I have left her to choose.

For what becomes of them has *never* mattered. You are the only One who matters.

> Alone I could not be
> For Thou hast been with me —
> To Mansions of Mirage
> In Fatal Equipage
> Called Back — O Muse,
> Master!

Author's Afterword

This fiction is based, with some variation and compression, upon actual events. In the words of Emily Dickinson's poem, I have tried to "Tell all the Truth" about her inner life, especially during her formative years at school; but I have chosen to do so in the "slant," fictional way that she herself preferred.

All the characters who write letters really existed. Emily Dickinson did spend just under ten months at Mount Holyoke Seminary in South Hadley, Massachusetts, from 1847 to 1848. The school's founder and headmistress, Mary Lyon (1797–1849), was, indeed, not pleased by Emily's failure to respond to the evangelical fervor that swept the seminary during the Second Great Awakening. An English teacher named Margaret Mann did read Milton with girls in Emily Dickinson's class, although nothing is known of her life after she left the seminary, shortly after Emily herself left. Because it was common knowledge that Emily's compositions provoked annoyance and envy among both teachers and classmates, I have imagined Miss Mann as hostile to her and I have conceived her as a type of the would-be poets and literary experts who scorned Emily Dickinson's work during — and after — her lifetime.

With the exception of Emily Norcross, the names of her schoolmates at Mary Lyon's are not recorded in Emily Dickinson's letters; so I have taken them from student lists in the Mount Holyoke College archives of the period.

Emily did room with her older cousin Emily Norcross, the daughter of her mother's brother Hiram; this Emily died, unmarried, in 1852 at the age of thirty-four. Abiah Palmer Root, born in 1830 like Emily Dickinson, was among Emily's closest friends until she married the Reverend Samuel W. Strong of Westfield, Massachusetts, in 1854. Before the wedding, she broke off their correspondence. There is no evidence that Abiah wrote to Susan Gilbert Dickinson (1830–1913) after Emily's death, although a few early friends did do so. I have imagined Abiah from the two dozen letters written to or about her by Emily Dickinson; and I have conceived her as I believe she was: the forerunner to Susan in Emily's passionate heart. (These letters, like the very few written during 1847–1848 at Mary Lyon's, may be found in *The Letters of Emily Dickinson*, edited by Thomas H. Johnson.)

It is true that Emily Dickinson left Mary Lyon's Seminary before completing the curriculum. The real chronology is more extended than the novel's. She returned to Amherst, unwillingly but unwell, in late March, not long after one of Miss Lyon's conversion assemblies. She remained at home until May 11, returned to Holyoke for a last semester, and left in August for good. Her family offered various explanations for Emily's departure, including homesickness, physical debility, and her discomfort at the Puritan discipline of the place. Emily's frail health probably caused Edward Dickinson to bring (and keep) her home. But I believe that such pressures as I envision taxed her health unduly and I have permitted myself to take seriously — and to dramatize — Emily's words about her failure to conform at Mount Holyoke: "I am not happy." The episode in which Emily refuses to number herself among the "Saved" and "declare for Christ" has its foundation in family memoirs. Although Mary Lyon was not known to have expelled unbelievers, Richard Sewall acknowledges that she "terrified" Emily Norcross and other girls by urging them to declare for Christ.

Lavinia Dickinson (1833–1899) liked to tell how Emily astonished her mathematics teacher with a solution she had never been taught. The theft of hundreds of cakes at Holyoke did take place in 1847, when Emily had the duty of polishing knives in the school refectory. An account of it (and of daily life at the school) may be found in the "Mount Holyoke Journal," written by a junior mistress and included in Jay Leyda's *The Years and Hours of Emily Dickinson*. There is no evidence that Emily was involved in this theft; but because her letters to Austin Dickinson (1829–1895) from the seminary harp upon sweets, and upon hunger — actual and symbolic, spiritual and carnal — I have made her the ringleader. It is thought that a postmaster named "Dickinson" delivered all the valentines; but, based on an ambiguous letter from her to Austin, I have imagined that Emily did. She did call herself "Eve" and the habit did provoke comment.

Emily's sister probably introduced her to Susan Huntington Gilbert: the woman who became her best friend, her sister-in-law, the heroine (and antiheroine) of a number of her love poems, and the person whom she best loved and by whom she was most hurt. We do not know whether Sue visited Emily at Holyoke, although they spent a great deal of time together subsequently. Sue's engagement to Austin actually took place in 1853, not 1848; but Emily had begun to ponder the consequences of it much earlier. Their reading of Henry Wadsworth

Longfellow's novel *Kavanagh* did not take place until 1849, when Austin Dickinson smuggled the novel into the Dickinson house as soon as it was published. (It was probably in that year, rather than 1848, that Emily read *Jane Eyre* as well.) My interpretation of Emily's relationship with Sue is based upon Dickinson's letters, Sue's letters (preserved in the Houghton Library of Harvard University), and on the biographical material presented by Richard Sewall in *The Life of Emily Dickinson* and by me in *The Passion of Emily Dickinson*. Susan's poem "Amor," which appears in Chapter LVIII, was indeed written by Susan Dickinson and may be seen in the Houghton collection in a cache of her scribblings that imitate Emily's poems and drawings, sometimes with comments about Emily herself on the same page. That Emily Dickinson's education continued long after her Holyoke days, we know from her letters to her affable, bemused, well-meaning literary mentor and first editor, T. W. Higginson (1823–1911). In them she describes an acquaintance with literature and art that is both deep and sophisticated. But her most profound affinity (after the Bible) was with Shakespeare. Therefore it is striking to read her words to Sue three years before she died: "Dear Sue — With the exception of Shakespeare, you have told me of more knowledge than any one living — To say that sincerely is strange praise."

It is not established nor has it ever, to my knowledge, been suggested that Mary Lyon was a lesbian in the contemporary sense of the word. There was no Eustacia. She did enjoy several exalted relationships with women, not unusual among unmarried Victorian schoolmistresses. She never enjoyed a privileged childhood; but it was one of her persistent dreams that she had, and she had a sensible attitude toward money as a means of achieving freedom. It is true that she usually wore white, as Emily Dickinson did later. In describing her convictions and manner of speech, I have been faithful to the portrait of her provided by Edward Hitchcock in a biography owned by the Dickinsons, *The Power of Christian Benevolence, Illustrated in the Life and Labors of Mary Lyon*. The rules and routines of the seminary are described in Elizabeth Alden Green's study *Mary Lyon and Mount Holyoke, Opening the Gates*. Lavinia Dickinson, always straightforward, said about Miss Lyon's establishment during Emily's time, "There were real ogres [there] then." Although the headmistress was personally kind, she had a reputation for severity as a principal.

Events and relationships such as the love affair between Austin Dickinson and Mabel Todd or the strife between Lavinia and Mabel over Austin's will are documented in Sewall, in Leyda, and in Polly Longsworth's *Austin and Mabel*.

Finally, there are two other matters of fact that I have altered here for symbolic reasons. Edward Dickinson was not as rich in 1847 as he would later become, nor was he ever as wealthy in fact as he is in Miss Mann's and Miss Lyon's imaginations. Nevertheless, the "Squire" was a powerful man of substance, which affected the lives of many, especially his daughter. There is one Dickinson house in this novel, recognizable as the Homestead on Main Street, now a shrine to the poet. But in 1847, the Dickinsons inhabited a house on North Pleasant Street. In November, 1855, they moved to the Homestead. There Emily died. Because her house was the symbolic refuge of Emily Dickinson's imagination, however, I have envisioned only the Main Street house, celebrated in her poems and letters.

As a girl, Emily Dickinson wrote the rather florid prose characteristic of the late eighteenth and early nineteenth century in New England. As she grew older, her style became that highly charged but austere language we think of when we think of her. I have tried to suggest that difference in her letters here, several of which incorporate sentences she herself wrote; and I have — blasphemously but lovingly — improvised examples of her poetry. Only ten poems are hers or include her lines. The last quatrain of "It makes no difference abroad," the final stanza from "This Consciousness that is aware," the first quatrain of "To fight aloud," and all of her poem "The Brain — is wider than the Sky" appear in Chapters XXXV, LXI, XXVII, and LXIV, respectively. I have quoted one line from "The Guest is gold and crimson" in Chapter XXV, three lines from "With thee, in the Desert" in Chapter LV, and three lines from "What I see not, I better see" in Chapter XLVI. Two lines from "I had been hungry, all the Years," two lines from "Mine Enemy is growing old," and one from "My wheel is in the dark!" are cited in Chapters XX, LXVI, and XXXIX. Margaret Mann paraphrases Emily's line "I'm Nobody! Who are you?" in Chapter IX. I have represented the poems quoted by others — Miss Mann, Higginson, Lavinia — in the forms in which each would have seen them. So when Miss Mann quotes "To fight aloud, is very brave" in Chapter XXVII, she represents the poem with the amended punctuation and line breaks supplied by Higginson and Mrs. Todd for the 1890 *Poems*. Lavinia, on the other hand, reproduces "The

Brain — is wider than the Sky" in the form she would have met in Emily Dickinson's handwritten copy. These handwritten poems may be imagined from facsimile volumes of the fascicle poems, edited by Ralph Franklin and called *The Manuscript Books of Emily Dickinson*. My improvised poems imitate Dickinson's arrangements in the fascicles.

Three characters in this novel — Sue, Higginson, and Mrs. Todd — consider Emily Dickinson's style faulty and in need of revision because of its inventive meters, rhymes, and metaphors. That is true to life. It illustrates the ignorance that marked Dickinson's treatment as a writer from the time she was a pupil at school up to, and sometimes subsequent to, the publication of the first collection of her poems in 1890 and the second and third collections in 1891 and 1896. It reminds us that genius requires freedom to explore its own vision, and that such "freedom" is really an inspired perception of form. Debate about how to print Emily Dickinson's poetry persists to this day. Some scholars argue that her verse should be published just as she copied it into the manuscript books. Others prefer the quatrains (metrically regularized but preserving Dickinson's eccentric punctuation) established by Thomas H. Johnson in the *Complete Poems*.

Of the "solutions" I provide to two of the several mysteries in this novel — the character of the daguerreotype-maker who made the only known photograph of Emily Dickinson, and the identity of "Master" — the first is merely playful. But in the second, I heartily believe.